For Mom

Contents

Dedication   ii

Foreword   iv

About the Authors   v

Chapters

1	An Introduction to Activities	1
	Guiding Principles for Activity Development	3
	Specific Considerations	3
	Ways of Making Contact	5
	Storytelling and Discussion as Cognitive Activities	6
	About Using the Term "Dementia"	7
	Building An Activity Session with Themes and Stories	8
2	Complex Stories for Normal and High Functioning Elders	10
3	Straightforward Stories for Mid-Level and Lower Functioning Elders	62

Additional Resources

The Five Big Hints (10 Examples)	123
Appendix A Infusing Interventions into Individualized Care: A Hierarchy of Goals	145
General References (alphabetically by first author)	146
General Footnotes (by Chapter)	150
Index of Terms	151
Order Form and Information	153

Foreword

My husband, Toby, and I went to see the movie Lourdes (2009) last week. The title of Jessica Hausner's movie makes it sound like a dedication to religious enlightenment and faith, but the story is not elevated or mystical. It is a story about everyday people: honest, curious, and very human.

Seemingly miraculous and unimaginably tragic events do happen in human life, and it is authentic to wonder about them. Tales of miracles and tragedies are not new, and they do fascinate us. Through the ages, people have told stories about giants (like the Nephilim, or Telmia, of the Old Testament), heroic acts, and unbelievable events. Those narratives are hard to believe, and it is difficult for the average person to identify with them. **Overall, the stories and poems in this book are not about fantasy worlds and giants. They are everyday fiction—not real, but written to sound like events and people in daily life. Sometimes, the best stories are those that sound as if they might have actually happened.**

Lauren Smerglia Seifert
June, 2010

About the Authors

Lauren Smerglia Seifert and Virginia L. Smerglia both bring considerable experience in aging research and in teaching to this endeavor. In two previous books, Lauren wrote about the psychology of aging and about activities for elders. Her practical work and her research aim to provide cognitive maintenance for elders with and without dementia. With a background in memory research and aging, Lauren has spent more than twenty years trying to understand memory change in aging and dementia. Moreover, since 1987, she has spent many hours in long-term care settings guiding activities for elders. Reference citations for Lauren's work are listed at the end of this book and include:

- Seifert & Jones, 2011
- Seifert, 2009 (book)
- Seifert & Baker, 2009
- Seifert, 2007 (book)
- Seifert & Baker, 2003
- Seifert, 1999

Virginia's work is in sociology—focusing on caregiving for older family members. She brings twenty-five years of teaching and research experience in gerontology to this project, and she was trained by noted gerontologist Charles Baressi. Virginia' s insights about families and aging are valuable and guiding. Selected references to her authorships also can be found at the back of this book. Examples are:

- Smerglia, Miller, Sotnak, & Geiss, 2007
- Miller, Smerglia, & Bouchet, 2004
- Smerglia, Deimling, & Schaefer, 2001
- Smerglia, 2000
- Smerglia & Deimling, 1997

1

An Introduction to Activities

This book describes activities for adults—particularly for elders. It is designed for activity professionals and caregivers who seek storytelling and activity techniques. Intended as a resource for caregiving of normal and high-functioning adults (Chapter 2) and for those with moderate-to-low cognitive functioning (Chapter 3), this book presents methods, ideas, and stories. Themes and topics include activities of adult life, inter-generational episodes, and reminiscence. A primary focus is on adulthood after mid-life, but many of the stories include multiple ages: from childhood, through mid-life, and into the later years.

The focus of the book is on storytelling—a very important part of adulthood and of the aging experience. **However, this book is not just a collection of stories.** ***It also includes techniques for guiding elder activities that provide enjoyment while supporting memory function.*** These methods are based on Lauren's research in the long-term care setting and the studies of other gerontologists. They are also rooted in both our experiences working in the field of gerontology, and in Virginia's background, which includes caregiving research.

About using memory and problem-solving tasks to help thinking and remembering (what scientists call "cognitive maintenance and enrichment activities"), hard science has not caught up with peoples' desires to build better activities, so that elders "think better for longer." Yet, a little bit of research does indicate directions for growth (e.g., Seifert & Baker, 2009). Among those directions is an approach to activities called "Practicing Against Decline" (or **PADding**; Seifert, 2009). It provides a foundation for some of the tasks in this book. In the PADding technique, we build a "scaffold" that supports better functioning (like using a large sign that is posted in a main hallway to signal an important event; about "scaffolding," see Vygotsky, 1926/1997). Then, we use scaffolding cues, paired with practice that is once-per-week over at least six weeks (Baker & Seifert, 2007; Seifert & Baker, 2009; Seifert & Jones, 2011). PADding provides a chance for better remembering, and some people have shown modest benefits from the approach (Seifert, 2007a; Seifert, 2007b).

For a number of years, Lauren and her colleagues (e.g., Seifert & Baker, 2009) have been talking about the **Six Week Rule** for practice/rehearsal in dementia care activities. We have found that participants with Alzheimer-type dementia or related memory impairments seem to improve their performance on some memory tasks when those tasks are repeated weekly for 6 weeks or more (e.g., pantomime recognition, Seifert, 1999; Seifert & Baker, 1998; Seifert & Baker, 2009). On some tasks, improvements manifest later—appearing after six months or more (Seifert & Baker, 2009). Other authors have talked about the importance of repetition for remembering (Ebbinghaus, 1885/1964), and of repetition with *active retrieval* when a person is being "tested" or "questioned" about something (Roediger & Karpicke, 2006). Repetition and active remembering might be very helpful, overall. Moreover, for persons with dementia, there might be a memory benefit in asking him/her to *perform an activity* (called "**subject-performed tasks**," like making a cup of tea; Rusted, Ratner, & Sheppard, 1995; Rusted & Sheppard, 2002). For some people, performing a task numerous times across days, weeks, and even months (with help, if needed) might be beneficial for memory (Seifert, 2009).

Keep subject-performed repetition in mind when you are developing activities; Lauren and her colleagues have seen some success (with small sample sizes) in their research on subject-performed tasks. In one activity called "Magazine Treasure Hunt," each participant searched through a magazine or catalog on his/her own. The group leader called out an item for everyone to search for (like "dog"), and results indicated that participants improved on the task from week-to-week, even though they were searching through different magazines/catalogs from one week to the next (Seifert & Baker, 2009). Over six *months* of participation, individuals with dementia showed improvement on the task—even though they had not shown significant gains during the first few weeks (see Seifert & Baker, 2009).

In applying the principles of **PADding**, the **Six Week Rule**, and **subject-performed tasks** to her storytelling activities, Lauren does the following:
- reads different stories each week but employs similar procedures, so that participants become familiar with "what will happen" in the storytelling activity.
- uses the storytelling activity on the same day of each week.
- starts each week's storytelling activity by writing, "Telling a Story" on the whiteboard at the front of the room.
- allows participants to read portions of the story aloud if they want to do so (a good way of making the task "subject-performed").
- allows participants to interject their own narrative, such as examples from their own lives that are related to the story.
- presents a crossword puzzle or an acrostics puzzle with clues and words from the story. This task comes after she reads the story, and the procedure is always the same—with Lauren giving clues and writing correct answers on the whiteboard at the front of the activity room. Typically, participants speak up with their responses as Lauren provides hints aloud and on the whiteboard.
- uses the same procedures each week for six weeks or more. Sometimes, she even uses the same task once per week for six *months* or more. Lauren varies the stories, but keeps the techniques within the storytelling activity session the same (e.g., always welcoming people, telling the story first, then using a trivia game or word game to build in repetition of ideas from the story). However, she doesn't use the storytelling task more than once per week with the same person(s). It's key to keeping the balance between practicing-against-decline and boring higher functioning participants!

- recycles a story (e.g., reading "What's Bluing?" once in March and once in May).

Guiding Principles for Activity Development

Planning activities for elders begins with knowledge about aging and about the specific elders for whom you help provide care. Whether you are an activity director, staff member, or a family member who is caring for an elder, the same basic principles can apply.

Find ways to build joy through the *personal history* and preferences of individuals for whom you provide care. This is called *person-centered* care, and it focuses on the person, rather than just on the activity (Kitwood, 1993). If it is no longer possible to engage in a cherished activity (e.g., golf, tennis, pottery, sewing), then find tasks that *include the subject matter, without requiring the declined skills.* For example, an avid golfer might still be able to practice putting, even if his/her days of "playing 18 holes" are over. A lady who loved to work on fine needlework might no longer be able to spend those hours bent over linen with a fine needle, making tiny stitches. However, she might enjoy going through a treasure trunk of her handiwork and explaining how to make the various types of stitches. A photo album of cherished counted, cross-stitch works might provide a wonderful focal point for one-on-one interactions and reminiscence.

Points of entry for enjoyment *need not be the exact activity as it was enjoyed previously*. Instead, enjoyment might begin with reminiscence about an activity, or by engaging in a modified task that includes the subject of interest. Lauren once worked with a lady who had been accomplished as a pianist. Severe arthritis kept her from playing, but it did not keep her from enjoying the work of others. Together they would sit and talk about the intricacies of various pieces—how one might bring out a subtle variation in a Mozart concerto, or the ways that Tchaikovsky might be expressed through the methods of striking the keys. Listening to piano music or recordings brought great joy! In this case, the discussion could reinforce self-esteem, too (see Appendix, Level 5).

Specific Considerations

People change throughout adulthood, and aging can be accompanied by shifts in a person's senses, perceptions, thinking, attention, physiology, social connections, and more. Many researchers have evaluated the potential for change from the early twenties into the nineties. A number of developmental trajectories have been plotted from age 25 to 75 (Blumberg, 1996; Goldman, 1970; both as cited by Hooyman & Kiyak, 2011). Those changes can include:

(1) lower visual acuity; more glare; and more yellow than was seen in younger years (Foos & Clark, 2008; Arking, 1991). It can also be more difficult to focus on objects as they approach or move away (Foos & Clark, 2008). From the mid-forties, the lens of the eye *accommodates* less well—meaning that it is less flexible and less able to focus

on small details and things that are nearby (Bjorklund, 2011);
(2) greater difficulty picking speech out of a noisy environment, and problems understanding fast speech (Tun, 1998)—also, trouble hearing higher pitches (after age 30; Bergman, 1971);
(3) a dulled sense of smell (i.e., after age 60; Doty et al., 1984);
(4) loss of muscle mass, bone mass, muscle strength and slowed reaction times (see Hooyman & Kiyak, 2011; Arking, 1991; Bjorklund, 2011);
(5) increases in total body fat (as discussed by Hooyman & Kiyak, 2011); and
(6) for some people, but not all, noticeable thinking and memory changes (as in dementia and neurocognitive impairment; Seifert, 2007; Seifert, 2009).

However, aging can also bring improved mood and emotion regulation (Lockenhoff & Carstensen, 2004). It is very often characterized by *stability* in personality—as is adulthood, in general (Deary, Weiss, & Batty, 2010). Aging can bring increased knowledge about words and their meanings (Verhaeghen, 2003). Too, crystallized intelligence (or factual knowledge) can increase up to around age 60, or very possibly throughout the entire life span (see Lindenberger & von Oertzen, 2006; Schaie, 2005; Hillier & Barrow, 2011). **Thus, aging is not simply diminishment.** An interesting set of studies indicates that a lot of what *seems to be "lost" intelligence in old age is actually a diminished capacity to take in information by way of one's senses, like vision and hearing* (see Baltes & Lindenberger, 1997). Can you imagine how different the world would be if people interacted with elders first and foremost *in an effort to be heard and seen*, rather than in ways that assume cognitive impairment?

Development continues throughout the lifespan, and moving past middle-age can bring both declines (as with hearing high pitches), as well as increases (such as having higher marital satisfaction and a sense of more freedom when one's children leave home; Antonucci, Tamir, & Dubnoff, 1980). Moving into the years past 80 might bring special challenges (like an increased risk of Alzheimer-type dementia; American Psychiatric Association, 2001), but those years can also stimulate great joy—like seeing great-grandchildren grow and mature, building new relationships, and discovering new activities for which one had no time when s/he was younger.

Planning activities for elders, then, must start with an idea that an elder's senses and skills can be *qualitatively and quantitatively different than when s/he was in young adulthood or middle age*. Principles to guide activity planning should include:
(1) less emphasis on smell and scents;
(2) improved lighting that reduces glare and increases contrasts (e.g., natural light from sky lights or through windows that can be shaded);
(3) visual aids that do not emphasize small visual details, but which *do accentuate the outlines of things, so that figures can be easily seen against their backgrounds*;
(4) sound cues that are clear and that do not emphasize high-pitched tones or high-pitched voices;

(5) activities that do not necessarily depend on quick movements or reactions; and
(6) activities that are appropriate for the cognitive skills of the adult—without being demeaning. Appropriateness includes "age appropriateness" (i.e., generally, having content that is fitting for adults and that is not childish). There are a number of excellent books on adulthood and aging, which can be consulted for more information about development across adulthood (e.g., Arking, 1991; Bjorklund, 2011; Foos & Clark, 2008; Hooyman & Kiyak, 2011; Hillier & Barrow, 2011).

Ways of Making Contact

Up to this point, we have implied some of the areas of contact in activity planning—by discussing ways that people stay the same and change in adulthood. Now, we must direct our attention to the *ways that we can make contact with an elder through activities*. "Domains of Contact" (or "ways of making contact") in eldercare are the same as those in our other interpersonal relationships. We make contact with people through:
(1) senses;
(2) emotions;
(3) memories and thoughts;
(4) spiritual aspects; and
(5) physical movements.

When you plan an activity, pay attention to the ways you will connect with the participant(s). For whom is this activity planned? Are you emphasizing "domains of contact" that will be effective for this person or persons? For instance, using sound as a primary domain of contact for someone who has profound hearing loss will probably lead you both to frustration—without success. For an elder with hearing loss, using vision or touch might be better.

Consider the following example as you think about how to connect with people. Lauren recently built a trivia activity for individuals with memory loss (Seifert, 2009). In the Five Big Hints task, participants are asked to follow along as the activity leader provides a category and clues. As the hints are given, participants try to guess the item/animal/person that is specified by them (e.g., ANIMAL, is a large bird, has beautiful plumes, "as proud as a _____").

At one facility, Lauren was unsuccessful including a resident who has profound hearing loss. The elder wanted to be around others, but once the activity would start, she would become very frustrated, because she could not hear the clues. So, Lauren started using PowerPoint® slides to supplement the spoken hints (see her article about this in *Activities Directors' Quarterly*; Seifert & Jones, 2011). Each hint was spoken *and shown on the screen*.

For each item in the Five Big Hints activity, Lauren used one slide with animation on "mouse clicks" (or by hitting the "Enter" key on her laptop). She started with the category of the item (e.g., ANIMAL, FURNITURE, VEGETABLE). Then, she could bring up a new clue on the slide, simply by clicking the mouse.

Well, the previously frustrated lady with hearing loss is now an engaged member of the Five Big Hints activity! She sits in the front row, reads the presentation slides, and periodically shouts out answers. The salient *visual cues* on the slides make up for her inability to hear the verbal cues. It is an illustration that domains of contact are VERY IMPORTANT to the success of your activities and to the well-being of participants. If all these clues were *only spoken* a participant with hearing loss might be unable to take part.

About the presentation, using a black background with cerulean-blue font for the text is the best display for simple hints on PowerPoint® slides (Seifert & Jones, 2011; in Calibri or Verdana font, sized "36" or larger; with font types as recommended through the teaching institute at eTeaching.eCollege.com). A projector mounted on the ceiling (or, at least, kept out of reach of participants) can be directed to shine on an activity room whiteboard or on a white wall. The glare is minimized, and participants' attention is drawn to the slides. Some facilities have televisions which can be used as computer monitors. In such cases, the TV might work as a display screen. However, this should only be attempted if the screen is large (43 inches X 27 inches or larger) and if glare can be minimized. Otherwise, one runs the risk that the slides will be too difficult for participants to see.

In a Five Big Hints slide show, one hint is presented at a time, and the simplicity of the slides holds participants' attention, without confusing them. After all the hints for an item have been given, a click of the mouse brings up a slide with a pleasing picture or photo of the item and its name (Seifert & Jones, 2011). Lauren uses custom artwork, because it's important for the visual images to be pleasing to the eye. That way—even if a participant does not guess correctly—s/he is rewarded for taking part, because the pictures are fun to view!

For complete details about how to build a PowerPoint® presentation, see the article in *Activities Directors' Quarterly* (Seifert & Jones, 2011). For more activities and the Five Big Hints, see Lauren's 2009-book and the back of this book. For information about the PowerPoint® presentations that Lauren has used, see our publisher's website at www.clovepress.com and "click" on "Contact Us."

Storytelling and Discussion as Cognitive Activities

Activities that we have constructed and tested in eldercare and dementia care are *not just fun*, they are also *cognitive*. They utilize thinking and memory. They are what some might call "cognitive exercise." In scientific articles, cognitive exercise is called "cognitive maintenance" and "cognitive enrichment" (e.g., Herzog, Kramer, Wilson, & Lindenberger, 2008). "Cognitive maintenance" happens when a specific skill or memory is preserved while a person's overall cognitive function declines. "Cognitive enrichment" is a general term for anything that can enhance thinking and memory.

We all want to believe there are ways to exercise memory and thinking so that they remain intact and healthy. To date, though, the jury is still out about how to achieve effective cognitive maintenance and/or enrichment. Psychologists have known for a very long time that practice through re-learning (such as learning a list of words and then re-learning the list a week later) can lead to better remembering (Ebbinghaus, 1885/1964). We experience something called "savings" when we try to re-memorize something we had learned previously. A kind of re-learning occurs when one is repeatedly tested on something—being asked to generate the information over and over again. This seems to lead to cognitive maintenance of the information (Roediger & Karpicke, 2006). Thus, for persons who have memory difficulties, repeatedly engaging in an activity that leads to "generating" the answers might be helpful (Seifert & Baker, 2009).

In a monograph on the subject, Herzog et al. (2008) argued for caution. Although there are some small-scale studies that show specific memories being maintained (e.g., Seifert & Baker, 2009), there are no large-scale trials that show big effects of practice on memory in dementia/cognitive decline. For now, the best we can do is to use what we know from basic memory research and what we have gathered from small-scale studies of cognitive maintenance and apply them in an effort to keep people's memories functioning effectively for longer. That's what the storytelling activities in this book (and the other activities in Lauren's previous books; Seifert, 2007; Seifert, 2009) are all about: using what we know about memory and thinking in order to help keep elder memory skills going. Do we *know that all these techniques work?* Well, Lauren and her colleagues have seen them work in some settings with some people. However, as we mentioned above, the jury is still out in the scientific community about just how big these effects are. For now, we remain convinced that active engagement in cognitive activities *can be recommended* for elders, both with and without dementia, because these activities are meaningful, are enjoyable, and have the potential to maintain or improve remembering. Moreover, many of the activities we recommend are social, too, leading participants to interact with each other in positive ways.

About Using the Term "Dementia"

We have mentioned dementia and cognitive deficits in previous paragraphs. Certainly, these are things that a caregiver or an activity staff member might encounter when building activities for elders. According to the American Psychiatric Association (2001; also called the "APA"), "dementia" is an ***acquired*** set of cognitive and memory deficits. "Acquired" means that the condition involves decline from a previous, higher level of functioning. Currently, the APA requires that the following be present for a person to receive a diagnosis of dementia: (1) a memory deficit of some kind; and (2) a movement, language, naming/recognition, or reasoning deficit (with specifications available in the DSM-IV-TR; APA, 2001). In addition, the deficits must affect a person's social functioning (i.e., in or out of the workplace; Kennedy, 2010). There are numerous diseases and conditions that are accompanied by dementia, and types of dementia can be different. For example, Parkinson's disease can be associated with a dementia that is quite different from the dementia found in Alzheimer's disease (Code 290.xx; APA, 2001). Thus, "dementia" is a very general term, which merely means that a person has identifiable decline in memory with a deficit in at least one other specified domain (as in #2, above; APA, 2001). Keep in mind that there are many different varieties of dementia.

The American Psychiatric Association (see Jeste et al., 2010) is planning to update "dementia" diagnoses. A new, general term—"neurocognitive impairment"—will most likely replace the term "dementia," and those conditions that are now associated with a diagnosis of "dementia" will be called "neurocognitive disorders." If this new term comes into use (in the new DSM-5 in May, 2013; APA, 2011), it will be associated with conditions in which (1) memory has declined from a previous level of functioning and, (2) cognition has declined in at least one other domain (such attention, planning and organizing one's activities, learning, vision-to-movement orientation, language, or interacting with people; see Jeste et al., 2010; Kennedy, 2010). In addition, the diagnosis of "neurocognitive disorder" will be further described as "major" or "minor"—depending on the degree of cognitive decline that a person has experienced (Jeste et al., 2010), and the criterion of "acquired" (as explained above) will continue to be part of the diagnosis. We mention these issues, because a few readers might be unfamiliar with APA diagnostic criteria and the potential changes in terminology. Notice that "neurocognitive impairment" implies that a person's memory and cognitive troubles probably carry an underlying neurological cause.

Building an Activity Session with Themes and Stories

Building useful activities for elders involves knowledge and creativity. Know the people, environment, and constraints in the setting where you are building activities.

(1) Use what you know about the person(s) for whom you provide care. Has someone been an avid quilter? Coin collector? Golfer? Traveler? This kind of information can help you to build "themes" (topics) into your activities with an individual.

(2) Use what you know about the time of year. Is it winter in Vermont? Then, build an activity about snow and activities of wintertime. Is it Hanukah in a Jewish community? Then, build activities around the Festival of Lights. Is it springtime in a Christian community? Then, design activities with Lenten and Easter topics.

(3) Use what you know about the environment. Are you a caregiver for an elder who is aging "in place" (at home)? Think about the routines that need to be established (e.g., grooming, meals, sleeping). Build activities that make these tasks pleasant and that use the individual's own interests as springboards for enjoyment. Are you an activity director at a long-term care facility? Know what types of activities are permitted and cost-effective. Use themes and the available resources in new and creative ways.

AN INTRODUCTION TO ACTIVITIES

(4) Be sure to use what you know about *limitations* in the entire "system." Those include: participants' levels of functioning and/or health concerns, environmental barriers (like a locked dementia unit or the 10-inches of snow that are likely to keep you indoors), financial considerations, and timing (scheduling meals versus sleeping versus bathing versus watching the news). Also, as it relates to considering the whole "system" in which an elder exists, see the Appendix of this volume in which Lauren has suggested a hierarchy of intervention goals for person-centered eldercare (Seifert, 2007; Greenspan & Wieder, 1998).

(5) Build routines (practice) into activities, so that participants can come to future activities with familiarity. Even if they do not consciously remember the activities, participants with Alzheimer-type and related dementia can benefit from practice. Maintaining similar routines across different activity sessions can help. For example, a staff member might wear a birthday hat and walk the halls of the long-term care facility with a bunch of balloons every month. S/he could do this fifteen-minutes prior to the monthly birthday party for residents who have a birthday that month. While approaching various residents, the staff member might say, "It's [name of month]! Who has a birthday in [name of month]?" Once a resident or group of residents is approached, the staff member would repeat the utterance and add, "[Name of resident], it's [name of month]. Is your birthday in [name of month]?" This sameness across sessions serves to cue (hint) that this is a particular type of event, and although participants might not have explicit memory that this happened last month, they might have some familiarity that will help them orient to the event this time around. "Familiarity" can happen even without conscious awareness, and it can happen even for people with Alzheimer-type (and related) dementia.

Page 9

2
Complex Stories for Normal and High-Functioning Elders

The following stories are appropriate for adults who are normal functioning or who are high functioning with dementia, mild cognitive impairment (MCI), or minor "neurocognitive disorder." These stories can be used by a caregiver who is caring for an individual (e.g., in home). They are also fitting for use by activity staff in elder daycare and residential living for elders. Many of the stories might also be appropriate for use with other high-functioning adult populations (e.g., younger and middle-aged adults with developmental disabilities).

Ideas for their use include:
- Reading them aloud to an individual or a group.
- Providing copies to individuals to read on their own (without including pages like this one, which are instructions for caregivers).
- Reading the stories and discussing them as part of a "reading group."
- Building whole, themed activities around a story: such as "Greek Festival"—which could be an activity with Greek pastries (like baklava), music, and dance—during which the story, "Dinner in Santorini" could be read aloud.

About "Talking Points"

When you tell a story in an activity session, it is easy to lose your place. Someone might decide to interject a comment or a question, and you'll want to be respectful of his/her query and respond to it. A participant might ask, "Why did she go to Greece?" If you were in the middle of the story about Santorini, you might respond, "She went to Greece on a business trip." By then, you might have lost your place in the story. Thus, it can be useful to have a list of "talking points" for each story in order to help you get back on track. This is simply a list of the story's main events or topics. We have supplied them for you in this book; talking points appear after each story. We find that it is helpful to make a copy to have on hand while reading the story aloud.

Talking points can also be used to stimulate discussion after a story has been read. State a talking point aloud, and then ask a question about it, or turn it into a question. For example, among the talking points for the story about Santorini is: "Santorini is a beautiful place—with hues of blue and white…." To make this a discussion question, show a photo (like those available with this book). Then, ask: "What colors are most noticeable in this picture of Greece?"

The Stories

Note: The following story is written in the first-person voice (for example, using "my", "I", and "we"). To have stories written in different voices ("They did this" versus "I did that") can provide nice variety. Also, first-person makes it possible to use this in a "dramatic" reading, in which the group leader plays the role of "Joyce", who narrates this story about her daughter's adventure. Enjoy!

Dinner In Santorini: A Story About My Daughter
by Virginia L. Smerglia

My name is Joyce. I am fifty-eight years old. My husband is Richard. He is sixty. We live in a small town near Philadelphia. We have been married thirty-seven years and we have a daughter, Holly, who is thirty-four. We named her Holly because she was born on December 26th, the day after Christmas. It was a bright sunny day and she is a bright and sunny person. Holly isn't married. Like a lot of young people nowadays, she says there's plenty of time to think about marriage. When Richard and I were young, a thirty-four-year-old unmarried woman would have been known as an "old maid," but today, she is known as a career woman.

Holly is an administrative assistant for a big company that makes washers, dryers, refrigerators, and dishwashers. She does a lot of what secretaries used to do, but—to get this job—she had to go to college and take computer courses and business courses. So, she is not called a secretary. Holly loves being an administrative assistant at the appliance company, because she meets interesting people. She says that no two days are the same.

Richard and I feel blessed that Holly got a job she loves just a half hour from where we live. She has an apartment only a few miles from our home. So, we get to see her quite often, and we love being included in her life.

One morning in early September, Holly stopped by on her way to work. The weather report predicted a beautiful day, and I had offered to take her little dog, Hanky-Panky, for a long walk. I must say Holly looked just dazzling that morning. She had on a light peach-colored suit. It wasn't bright, but pale—kind of like the color of peach yogurt. Her long wavy ash blond hair was pulled back and she had on the brilliant sapphire earrings she got from Richard's mother—her grandma—on her eighteenth birthday. Oh, her shoes…she has a closet full of shoes. Her shoes were very high-heeled and matched the color of her suit exactly. I know a mother is prejudiced, but she really was, like I said, "dazzling." And, I couldn't help but think that she could take any young man's breath away.

Holly got to work early that morning and found the whole office was buzzing with a rumor that they were about to buy a large appliance company in Greece. She didn't think much about it because she had a pile of work waiting on her desk. So, she went in her office and closed the door. But, a few minutes later, her boss, an executive named Sheila, knocked on her door and said they needed to talk about the rumor. Holly listened. The company was sending Sheila, along with several other managers, to Greece to discuss buying the Greek company. Sheila wanted Holly to go along to assist her in the meeting.

Holly was so excited! A trip to Greece! She was thinking of what to take along when Sheila said, "We're leaving in an hour. Do you have your passport here at the office?"

"An hour," said Holly. "How ?"

"Well," Sheila said, "it seems our Greek colleagues have sent their corporate jet for us and that's when it will be here. So, do you have your passport?"

"I have it," Holly said. "Just let me call my parents and ask them to bring a suitcase. How many days will we be gone?"

"There's no need for a suitcase. We are only going for dinner," said Sheila.

"What?" Holly squeaked.

Sheila continued, "For dinner….we're going to Greece for a dinner meeting, Holly!"

Holly called us, but there was not much she could tell us because she had to leave. I said, "We'll take good care of Hanky-Panky, so you go have a good time!"

"Mom," she said, "this is a business meeting, not a good time!"

So, I said, "Whatever!" because that's what all the young people say when they have no more comment!

An hour later, Holly found herself on a corporate jet with big, comfy chairs and couches, all kinds of snacks and beverages, and soft music. It was surely nothing like traveling on a regular airline. A male flight attendant brought each of them a drink and a warm washcloth for their hands. Then he passed trays of little sandwiches, fruit, and Greek honey cookies. Meanwhile, there was serious conversation among the executives who would be negotiating with the Greeks. The pilot's voice came on and welcomed them in English. He said they would be landing on the Greek island of Santorini in four and a half hours. Their host would meet them on Santorini, at his home. The flight attendant would take care of anything they needed during the flight.

When the executives were finished meeting, Holly's boss, Sheila, talked with her about the meeting in Greece. She needed Holly to take notes on her laptop computer and also to be prepared to look up any information Sheila might need. Holly asked who their host was…whose home they were going to on the island. Sheila said the host was the owner of the Greek appliance company they wanted to buy. His name was Alexander Nellos. Sheila said they were all going to nap or read for the rest of the flight so they would be at their best. They had left in early morning. So, with the flight and the time change, it would be early evening, about 6:00 P.M., when they arrived on Santorini.

Later, when Holly awoke from her nap, she looked out the window. The pilot announced they were flying lower as they came in over the Aegean Sea. Holly looked on a most beautiful sight…that the sea sparkled like it was made up of millions of indigo blue jewels. The sky was the most crystal clear she had ever seen and she wondered how on earth the pilot could find the right landing spot among the many small islands below. But, find it he did and as they came closer, she saw Santorini looking like a

green crescent in the sea. The cliffs and hills rose from the water and the buildings on the slopes were all the whitest white imaginable. The sapphire sky, the indigo sea, and the white buildings looked unreal, like a painting.

Then, the plane landed on an airstrip and two cars transported them around the hillsides to Mr. Nellos' home. After they drove through the gate, the cars took them to a beautiful grape arbor. Rough wooden tables were set with bottles of red, white, and pink wine and trays of fruit and cheese. Chairs with puffy cushions were set about. But, the group was so awestruck by the views of the sea and the hillside vineyard, no one moved to sit down. Cruise ships in the harbor below looked small. And, they could see mules on the roads transporting vegetables and fruit to the harbor town below. Holly said all she could think was, "This morning I got ready for work like I do every other day and now I am in this beautiful place on an island in the Aegean Sea!"

The group heard someone calling "Hello, hello!" They looked in the direction of a large white-washed home. It was surrounded by gardens and trellises of flowers in every imaginable color. Alexander Nellos came toward them, with hands outstretched, calling, "Welcome, Friends! Welcome!" He shook each person's hand. There were six

of them including Holly and another administrative assistant. "Please, please, refresh yourselves and get some wine!" he said as he pointed to a small white building with a porch. It had a basket of towels and pitchers of drinking water. Holly assumed this would be a restroom they could use.

Mr. Nellos said, "We'll have a glass of wine and then a meeting before dinner."

The group from Holly's company was not accustomed to drinking alcohol before or during business meetings. In fact, that would be considered a "no-no" in their world. But, as Holly told me later, "We were definitely not in our world. In fact, it seemed maybe we were on a different planet." In any case, they could not be rude guests, so they took some wine and tried to sip slowly. After they had some cheese and fruit with their wine, Mr. Nellos led them to his home and into the conference room which was at the back of his house. The conference room was all windows, which were open onto the sea air. Holly thought this would be a business meeting like no other she had ever attended. She believed Mr. Nellos would do very well in any negotiations in this heavenly atmosphere. She couldn't imagine anyone disagreeing in this room.

There were nine chairs at the conference table. The group from Holly's company sat and Mr. Nellos said his son and their attorney would be there any minute to fill the two empty seats. Everyone prepared for the meeting, getting out their materials, and Mr. Nellos and the leader from Holly's company, Michael Trenton, passed around proposals. The door opened and in came Mr. Nellos' son, Joseph, and his attorney, Mr. Spirtos. Joseph took an empty chair next to Holly and introduced himself. Although Mr. Nellos had on casual clothes…a sweater…his son had on a light gray suit that complemented his gray eyes. He wore a pale peach tie the exact color of Holly's suit.

Holly later told us the meeting was a blur to her. She did everything Sheila asked, but she could not ignore the fact that Joseph was staring at her and talking to her at every opportunity. Finally, the meeting ended. Holly could only think about Joseph Nellos' gray eyes. Then, as if she had wished it, she found he was seated next to her at dinner, which was served in the home's beautiful gardens. Mr. Nellos' wife, Diana, also joined the group and Holly saw that Joseph looked like her, tall, slender, gray-eyed and graceful.

Dinner on Santorini Island, overlooking the harbor lit with hundreds of lights and under the sky, lit by millions of stars, was not only romantic, it was like something out of a movie. After dinner, they had an hour until their plane would depart. Joseph took Holly on a tour of the gardens. There were fountains with rainbow lights and pathways lined with tiny lights. The thousands of blossoms made the night air fragrant.

Joseph took Holly's hand and said, "You know, Holly, I am coming to the U.S. next week to continue the negotiations. I'll be there for a month. I would very much like you to show me Philadelphia and maybe even New York and Washington, if you have the time. I know it's a lot to ask, but I have a feeling we should get to know each other better. I have enjoyed these past few hours with you more than I can say."

Of course, my daughter, the career woman, looked into those gray eyes and said, "Oh, I have plenty of free time these next weeks. I will look forward to showing you whatever places you'd like to visit."

So, Holly flew home, came to pick up Hanky-Panky the next day, and told us this whole story. She and Joseph have now made many plans for his time in the U.S. He will be here in two days and, if the flowers and small gifts he has sent are an indication, I think the visit will go well. By the way, he even sent two bottles of wine for Richard and a book of Greek poetry for me! How about that?!!

- Joyce is the story's narrator, and her husband is Richard.
- They live in Philadelphia and have a grown daughter: Holly.
- Holly is the administrative assistant for an important business manager and she must go on a spur-of-the-moment business trip to Greece.
- Holly is always dressed "to the nines" because of her job. She loves shoes!
- Holly and her boss left Philadelphia in the morning and arrived in Santorini, Greece for a business dinner.
- Santorini is a beautiful place—with hues of blue and white. The sunset is lovely.
- On her adventure, Holly met a young man—Joseph Nellos—who is the son of a Greek business owner.
- There might be a budding romance between Holly and Joseph. Holly will "show him the town" when he visits Philadelphia in two days!

Kiki's Pictures
by Lauren Smerglia Seifert

Hot, white glare showed through the front windows of the store. It had been a blistering July in the city—even hotter inside the dry cleaning store. The east side of town was especially steamy in the mornings, when the dry cleaner was busiest. Bright sunshine fell across the street, bringing extra heat into the store from the sunlight's reflections off the pavement.

Mr. Gee would open the blinds at 7:00 A.M. each day of the week except Sunday. As he pulled the blinds open at each window, he would breathe deeply and say, "Kiki, it is going to be a fine day."

Kiki had worked for Mr. Gee for two years. The days were long and arduous, and Kiki was trying to save money for college. At eighteen, as a recent high school graduate, she wanted to study photography and art, but she would have to work a lot of extra hours at the dry cleaner to have enough money for her art school tuition. Mr. and Mrs. Gee had been very kind to Kiki—hiring her to help with deliveries and to process dry cleaning orders.

The city was so very hot that the Gee's had recently bought a cool little cabin up in the wooded hills east of town. It was their getaway from the city's scorching July days. In fact, they had just returned from a leisurely weekend away, during which they had trusted Kiki and her brother Monty to run the dry cleaning store. Everything had gone well, and Mr. Gee returned to the city happy and refreshed.

Monty, at twenty, enjoyed being a big brother to Kiki. However, most people considered the siblings to be like twins. Their silky black hair and beautiful dark eyes were similar. They were two of a kind, and they both worked very hard to save money for Kiki's education. Sometimes, people would ask Monty why he wasn't saving for his own schooling, and he would just smile—eyes twinkling. In his heart, Monty knew how talented his sister was, and he wanted her to have the chance to become an artist. He remembered her sixth birthday, when she had received her first camera. Even then, she had what most people call "an eye for beauty." Kiki could find a photo anywhere. She snapped pictures of lamps, toasters, dogs, and trees. Monty thought that each one of Kiki's photos seemed to capture the essence of its subject. Monty was content to save money for Kiki's art school tuition, because he knew she would be an amazing artist.

On that sunny Monday, an envelope arrived for Kiki. It was a response to her art school application from the College of Fine Arts. They had evaluated samples of her work. In the envelope was a letter from a Professor of Photography at the school. She had taken the time to write a letter to Kiki.

"Dear Kiki Alvarez," the letter began. "I regret that we cannot offer you a position in our incoming photography class this autumn. Your work shows great promise. However, it lacks something. Art comes from experience, and the samples of your work that we have reviewed seem to be confined to a small set of experiences and a small space—just city streets. I hope that you will consider applying to our institution in the future, but before you do, I recommend that you travel. Take some time to see the world and take pictures of it. Sincerely, Professor Beverly Porter."

Kiki frowned. As Monty searched her face to understand the contents of the letter, he realized that she had not been accepted. He took the letter from her and studied it. Then, he said, "Well, we've never been outside of the city. Our whole lives have been lived within fifteen blocks. If this professor wants you to travel, then we will find a way for you to do it."

Mrs. Gee had overheard Monty's voice as she came out of the storeroom. She smiled at Kiki and hugged her after Kiki read the letter to her. "Kiki, I know that it is hard to know how you will travel—with money being so tight. However, I think I know of a way for you to start your travels, take more photos, and start your journey toward an acceptance into art school."

Mrs. Gee walked away and went into the back room of the dry cleaning store, where Mr. Gee was working. Kiki and Monty could not hear the Gees' conversation, but they could hear its tone, which sounded very serious. After a few minutes, Mrs. Gee came back from the office with her husband. Mr. Gee said, "Monty, Kiki, this coming Saturday, the dry cleaning store will be closed. Pack some clothes for the weekend, because you are coming to the cabin with us. Kiki, bring your camera. There are a lot of photos to be taken in the hills!"

Kiki frowned. All she could think about was losing an entire Saturday's pay. She and Monty would both be at the cabin, and they would both be without wages for the weekend. As if he had read her mind, her brother touched her on the shoulder and said, "Kiki, sometimes experiences are more important than making money."

Looking at Mr. and Mrs. Gee with his handsome, dark eyes, Monty said, "Thank you so much, Mr. and Mrs. Gee. We will be ready at 7:00 A.M. Saturday morning. Thank you. Thank you!"

So it was, that early Saturday morning Kiki and Monty met the Gees in front of the dry cleaner. The sun was white-hot and bright, as they threw their overnight clothes into the trunk of the Gees' car and jumped into the back seat for the drive to the cabin.

Mrs. Gee asked, "Did you bring a sweater?"

Astonished, Kiki replied, "No. It is so hot. I think it will be near 96 degrees today!"

The Gees smiled at each other, and Mr. Gee winked. Kiki and Monty looked at each other with puzzlement. Neither of them could imagine why a person would need a sweater on a day that would be well over 90 degrees!

There was a lot of traffic on that Saturday morning as Mr. Gee drove their blue four-door sedan out of the east side of the city toward the outlying hills. Many people seemed to have the same idea: of getting away from the city. As the final weekend in July, this would be one of the last chances for families with children to get away before the new school year started. The Gees had one child, a daughter named Tamara, who had gone to Toronto to spend the summer with her aunts. Tamara was sixteen, and she would start working at the dry cleaning store when she returned from visiting her aunts' house in late August.

Two hours after they had left the city, the blue sedan was ascending a winding road that was shaded by very tall trees. As Kiki and Monty looked up, they were both amazed at how high the trees were and about how far up a person had to look—even to see the lowest branches. Having lived in the city all their lives, Monty and Kiki were accustomed to the occasional apple and cherry trees that city workers planted on median strips and along sidewalks. Such trees rarely grew very tall, and city trees tended to be shorter, with very low branches.

Unable to contain his surprise, Monty exclaimed, "The trees are so tall. I can't believe my eyes!"

Mr. Gee laughed and pulled the car over along a roadside berm. It looked as if many cars had been here before theirs. There were deep tire marks in the dirt between two trees. Mr. Gee remarked, "We call this 'two oaks lookout' and it is one of our favorite rest stops along the journey up to our little cabin."

The four travelers got out of the car after Mr. Gee put it in "park." Mrs. Gee beckoned to Kiki and took her hand. "Kiki, come with me. I want to show you something," Mrs. Gee said with a kind smile.

As they walked along a dirt path, the hill became very steep. Kiki imagined that it would be very difficult to walk up this hill in the rain, because it would be very slippery. Mrs. Gee squeezed Kiki's hand, as if to reassure her, and then, Kiki saw it: the hilltop. Coming up behind them, Monty gasped, "Woa! This is awesome!"

As they looked out from the spot where Mrs. Gee had stopped, Kiki and Monty could not believe the beauty. It was a tree-lined gorge through which a creek was running. There were more kinds of trees than either of the siblings knew existed! They were high enough that they could look into the limbs of the tall trees below and see birds and squirrels. There was an echo of birds singing their songs, and the sun was shining through the branches onto the creek bed below them.

Before anyone could suggest it, Kiki was snapping photos…of leaves, of the creek, of anything she could frame and focus. The scent of tree bark and water filled the air, and Monty proclaimed, "I never knew that water had such an awesome scent. It is so fresh. It smells clean. It is wonderful here!"

After a while, Mr. Gee suggested that they should be going. He reassured them, "Don't worry. There is a lot more to see up at the cabin."

They drove another twenty minutes up the twisting, shady drive until they came to an unmarked entrance. Mr. Gee turned left and followed the dirt road—going slowly and being careful to ease the blue sedan around deep ruts and over bumps in the long driveway. Then, as if it had appeared from nowhere, there was a little brown cabin of cedar and stone. Monty helped Mr. and Mrs. Gee unload some boxes of groceries and supplies from the car's trunk, while Kiki ran around taking photos. After a few minutes, Kiki walked in through the front door of the cabin and apologized, "I'm so sorry that

COMPLEX STORIES

I didn't help unload the car. There is just so much to see that I couldn't stop taking pictures of it all!"

Mrs. Gee laughed and replied, "Kiki, that's OK. That's why you're here. You are finding your inspiration."

That afternoon, Mr. Gee made hamburgers on the grill, and Mrs. Gee sliced watermelon and cantaloupe. Kiki and Monty helped set the picnic table out on the back porch, and the four ate heartily—enjoying the sounds of birds that called to each other through the woods. After lunch, Kiki and Monty followed a trail into the woods and Kiki snapped pictures as they went.

After an hour-long hike, Monty asked, "Have you ever seen anything so beautiful? Look up at that tree. It's leaves are shaped like mittens!"

"That is a sassafras tree, Monty," said Mrs. Gee, who was walking up behind them on the trail. She had brought a small bag with soda pop and binoculars in it. She continued, "Kiki and Monty, you should stop to have something to drink. Then, I'll show you the best place in all the woods!"

After a ten-minute break from their hike and a few sips of orange soda, Kiki said, "Let's hike some more. I want to see your favorite place in the woods, Mrs. Gee!"

On they went, through the trees and brush. Mrs. Gee led them toward a rushing sound: "Whoosh! Swoosh!" The sound became louder as they walked. Then, suddenly, they were looking down into a deep gorge. They were high above a rushing river. The water surged and gurgled below them, and the air whirled around in the riverbed.

"It's a very loud sound!" Monty said, astonished.

"Why, yes. Monty, nature can make a lot of noise!" Mrs. Gee replied.

Kiki chimed in, "It is so funny, because I always thought of the city as noisy. I thought that the woods must be very quiet, but they are noisy with birds, squirrels, wind, and rushing water. There is also a loud screeching sound. It is very high-pitched. What is it?"

Mrs. Gee laughed, and then she said, "Those are harvest-flies or cicadas [pronounced 'si-kay-duhs']. They are like locusts, and they screech from their perches high up in the trees during July and August, but Kiki, just wait until tonight. You'll hear sounds you've never imagined—frogs, crickets, and more!"

After Kiki took photos of the river, the three hikers made their way back to the cabin. Kiki and Mrs. Gee prepared a salad and some dinner rolls, while Mr. Gee showed Monty how to grill steaks. The four of them sat down to a delicious supper, and they listened to the sounds of the woods. As supper ended, it seemed to be getting dark. Monty was puzzled, and he asked "What time is it? It seems to be getting dark so early."

Mr. Gee chuckled after looking at his watch, "It's just 7:30 P.M., Monty, but the

TELMIA

days are shorter in the woods, because the trees hide the sunrise and the sunset. If you look straight up through the highest tree limbs, you'll notice that the sky above is still quite bright, but it is getting dark down here, because we are deep in the woods."

A chilly breeze came through the air, and Mrs. Gee came outside with sweaters for everyone. Even though the day had been hot, the night would be cool because of nature's air conditioning: the trees!

Mrs. Gee offered her daughter's bedroom for Kiki to sleep in, and Monty would sleep on the couch in the living room. As they prepared for bed, Mr. Gee closed up the doors and made sure that the windows were open and the window-screens secured with latches. Windows in the back of the house had double-mesh screens on them, and Monty asked why. Mr. Gee replied, "There's a raccoon who thinks he's part of our family. He used to let himself in through the back window, so I put double-mesh screens on the windows, in order to keep him out."

Monty was surprised. There were many things about the woods that he hadn't considered—like all the animals roaming around!

On Monday morning, back at the dry cleaning shop, the day was dawning hot and bright. It would be another blazing day in the city. Kiki and Monty had enjoyed their weekend vacation with the Gees. They were very grateful for the hospitality that their bosses had offered them. Kiki told Monty that she felt inspired by the woods and amazed by everything they had seen and heard. "I'm going to re-apply to art school with my new photos," she said.

Two months later, Kiki made a new portfolio with some pictures of the city and many new photos: a few that she had snapped outside the dry cleaner and many that she had taken in the woods during their weekend with Mr. and Mrs. Gee. Kiki sent the new portfolio to the College of Fine Arts, with a letter about her exciting experiences. She had been encouraged by the Professor's letter, and she was asking to be considered for January admission.

Three weeks later, there was a large, thick envelope waiting for Kiki on the counter in the dry cleaner's when she returned from the corner market with some groceries for Mrs. Gee. As the envelope caught Kiki's attention, she asked, "Is it for me? Is it from the College of Fine Arts?"

"Yes. Yes," Mrs. Gee answered. "Open it up, and let's see what it says!"

Opening the envelope, Kiki could see that it was filled with materials—papers and a booklet. On top of them was a letter from the same professor who had written to Kiki in July regarding her rejection. This time, the letter was very good news, Professor Porter had written, "Dear Kiki, It is my pleasure to offer you a place in our incoming class this January. Your new portfolio is impressive and greatly improved over the previous one. In particular, our admissions committee was stunned by the photo you have taken of two people standing outside a dry cleaning shop. It is as if you have captured their very being! Congratulations! I look forward to seeing you in my Introductory Photography course in January!"

Kiki was astonished. The photo of the Gees outside the dry cleaner's had been an afterthought—something she added to the portfolio—just to show that she could take pictures of people, too. However, she had thought that the College would be impressed by her photos from the Gees' cabin. Yet, those weren't mentioned at all!

In May, Kiki was finishing her first semester at the College of Fine Arts. As she completed her final project in Professor Porter's Introductory Photography class, their discussion turned toward portfolios. Professor Porter said, "Kiki your admissions portfolio had some very interesting work in it, but the most impressive photo was a picture of two people standing in front of a dry cleaning shop. It was astounding, and that is why the admissions committee accepted your application."

Still puzzled about that, Kiki said, "I'm surprised that it wasn't one of the photos from the woods that was preferred. You had suggested that I travel, and I thought my pictures of the cabin and the trees were very nice. The photo at the dry cleaner is just a picture of where I work."

"Ah, yes, Kiki," responded Professor Porter. "It is important to travel, if you can, because it is the experience of traveling which helps us to understand who we are. The photo at the dry cleaning shop is the best, because your heart is in it. After you went away from it, you were able to see it more clearly, and that is what helps to create the best pictures of all!"

As Kiki left Professor Porter's office, she thought about the photo of Mr. and Mrs. Gee standing in front of the dry cleaning store. She had taken the photo on Sunday afternoon, when they returned from the trip to the cabin. She and Monty and the Gees had been so happy, and they had shared a wonderful weekend. As she thought about the photo, she realized that Professor Porter was right. The trip to the woods had helped

Kiki to see much more clearly what had been in front of her all along: two people who cared for Monty and for her very deeply. Professor Porter could see that the dry cleaner's was where Kiki's heart was. The photo showed it. Only after she had been to the woods did Kiki truly see how important the city, the dry cleaner's, and the Gees were to her.

Talking Points for "Kiki's Pictures"

• Kiki and her brother Monty work for the Gees, who own a dry-cleaning store.
• Kiki and Monty work hard, but they do not have extra money.
• Both of them wanted to see Kiki gain acceptance to art school, so that she could become a photographer.
• Kiki's recent application to art school was denied, with a professor noting a lack of variety in Kiki's photos.
• The Gees wanted to help, so they took Kiki and Monty to their cabin outside the city.
• Along the drive to the cabin, they encountered interesting things, like a beautiful overlook from which you can see a tree-lined gorge. It is "two-oaks lookout."
• Once at the cabin, Kiki and Monty experienced many new things: like the fact that raccoons like to pry open the back screen in order to scavenge in the kitchen for food!
• They ate delicious meals and enjoyed the woods. They discovered that—even in the summer—days are shorter in the woods, because the trees hide the sunrise and the sunset.
• When they return to the city, Kiki is eventually admitted to art school. Her "best" photo is one featuring the Gees in front of the dry cleaning store.
• It is Kiki's trip away from the city which has given her a "new vision" in her photos—helping her to show tremendous expression in her photo of the Gees.

The Kissing Wall
by Virginia L. Smerglia

The town of River Bend is located at a beautiful point on the Ashland River. In fact, it is so beautiful that visitors to the town often say things like, "What a heavenly spot!" The surrounding hills are covered with forests and meadows. The trees change with the seasons and wildflowers and birds add every color. So, the views are heavenly!

As you might guess from the name, "River Bend," the town is in a place where the Ashland River curves. In fact, the river curves so much that the town is a peninsula. Part of the town faces east and part faces west. Some of the town's residents see the sun rise in the east and some see the sun set in the west. So, through the years, people have called these two areas of the town "Sunrise" and "Sunset." They're used to saying things like, "I live in Sunrise" or "I'm going to see friends over in Sunset."

The town's layout has stayed pretty much the same throughout its two-hundred-year history. This is because besides occupying a very beautiful spot, River Bend has been protected from floods. The Ashland River's current is not too swift, and the town sits a little above the river.

Part of the town is a park on the river bank in the Sunset area. This beautiful park, called Sunset Park, has been there about as long as the town. Here, the sunsets change according to the season. They tend to be pink and blue in spring and summer, golden and orange in fall, and blue and violet in winter. The sunsets in the park are so very beautiful that unless it is cloudy, there is usually an audience of town residents in cars and on park benches. It rests the mind and gives peace to the soul to sit there and watch the colors of the sky at sunset.

In the park, about two hundred feet back from the water's edge, is a stone wall which has been there as long as anyone can remember. The wall is made of smooth river stones of many colors: gray, brown, red, and even a sort of blue. It is about three and a half feet high.

There are some town legends about the wall. One is that the wall was built by early settlers to discourage large animals like bears from coming into town. The settlers believed animals would hunt further downstream rather than trying to get over or around the wall. It's interesting that there are no tales about whether the wall was a success at keeping animals out of town, but it is a tradition to refer to the wall's ability, like saying that something is as likely to happen "as a bear coming over the wall at sunset." When a town's person says such a thing, she or he means that something isn't very likely to happen.

A second tradition is that the wall is where young lovers share their first kiss. Of course, that's where the wall got its name. It is called "the kissing wall." Also, there have been many marriage proposals there. So, the wall is quite a romantic place and many couples have carved their initials into the trees nearby.

Angela and Kevin Thayer are one of the town's well-known couples who got engaged at the kissing wall. Angela is the forty-four-year-old mayor of River Bend. And, people love to say her name: "Mayor Thayer." If there's a problem, like too many mosquitoes in summer or too many chuckholes in winter, someone is sure to remark, "Well, what did Mayor Thayer thay?" And, Mayor Angela Thayer takes the joke in good humor.

TELMIA

Here's the story of Angela and Kevin and the kissing wall. Twenty-one years ago, on a beautiful warm July evening, Kevin Thayer showed up at Angela's house with a box of fast-food fried chicken and a bottle of champagne and asked if she would like to join him for a picnic supper in the park. She was twenty-three at the time and just finishing her first year as a junior accountant at the local hospital. She and Kevin had been high school sweethearts. Their college years separated them. They had been far apart, and they had dated other people. After college, they came home to find they were still soul mates.

So on this July night, Angela was a little shocked but very happy when Kevin, nervous and shaking, perched her on top of the kissing wall and brought out the champagne and a diamond ring. Angela was surprised, because Kevin had just finished his training at the police academy. That's right. He was a brand new policeman—on the job for only a few months. Angela thought he might want to get more experience in his new career before making any more big decisions. But, she later found out that Kevin was worried. He was afraid one of the young doctors at the hospital where she worked might ask Angela out and he thought a rookie cop couldn't compete with a doctor!

Now, twenty-one years later, Angela is the mayor of River Bend. She has been mayor for six years. Kevin is a detective in the police department, and they have two daughters, Mattie, age ten, and Della, age seven.

The thing that occupies Angela's mind these days is a very large dilemma for her and for the town council. They have decisions to make which could change their town and probably will change their town. These decisions concern the kissing wall. How can this charming stone wall which is an important part of the town's history be involved in a huge problem?

Well, the problem begins with a town resident named Carlos Cryan. That's right: Cryan. Mr. Cryan has always said he is the great-great-great-great grandson of one of the town's founders—a trapper named Keagan Cryan. Carlos says that because his ancestor was one of the two town founders, and because the park land is where they came ashore to found the town, the park belongs to him. Carlos Cryan and his attorneys claim the town must give the park to Mr. Cryan or go to court.

Mr. Cryan wants to take the kissing wall down and use the stones as part of a house he is building for himself. He claims that his great-great-great-great grandfather Keagan helped build the wall and, therefore, the stones in the wall belong to him. Furthermore, Carlos Cryan wishes to build a restaurant where the wall is and call it, "The River Rock Grill." Since he plans to hire an excellent chef to provide gourmet dinners, many families in River Bend will be unable to afford to dine there. The generations of enjoyment the park has brought could become just a memory.

The problems faced by Mayor Angela and her council are about the town's

COMPLEX STORIES

traditions and also about whether they can fight Mr. Cryan's claims. So, she and the council president, Darryl Jefferson, have called a council meeting. The town's council has come up with some solutions to the problems, and now, they must present the possible solutions in a meeting of town residents.

On the night of the meeting, tension mounts as the town hall fills with residents of all ages, from all areas of town. Carlos Cryan is not present. When Mayor Thayer gets to the podium and adjusts her microphone, her face is looking pale, but her husband Kevin is happy to hear her voice is strong as she calls the meeting to order.

She says, "I am proud to be a citizen of this town and I thank you for the privilege of being your mayor. My request is that we speak with respect for each other's opinions tonight. Council President Jefferson and I will present the possible solutions for our dilemma. The council members are here to answer questions during and after the meeting. I ask that you hear all four possibilities before you form an opinion and before you comment. Mr. Jefferson will present the first two solutions."

Darryl Jefferson takes the microphone and his voice seems a bit shaky. Darryl has lived his whole life on the Sunrise side of River Bend. His father was a hard-working janitor in the schools who was proud to have his son Darryl attend college and become one of the first male nurses at the hospital. In fact, Darryl is an excellent nurse whose patients are generally pretty happy to have his kind and devoted care. Early in his career, he got used to the jokes from his friends about being a male nurse, but now there are plenty of other men who are nurses at the hospital and he doesn't even think about it.

Tonight, he is wishing he were at the hospital or anywhere else instead of in front of this meeting. He and the mayor and town council have tried hard to think creatively about solving this problem. He hopes the citizens will be open-minded and not jump to conclusions.

Darryl speaks slowly. "Our first possible solution," he says, "is to do nothing." There is mumbling among the citizens as Darryl continues with, "Our town legal advisor tells us that Mr. Cryan cannot remove any of the kissing wall until he obtains a legal title to the land. He has not done that yet. He will have to prove that Keagan Cryan is his great-great-great-great grandfather. He will also have to show that Keagan had title to the park land and never sold it. So, if we do nothing, we will either end up losing the kissing wall and the park or not—depending on whether Mr. Cryan can prove his claims to a court and receive a judge's approval."

A few people raise their hands, but Darryl says, "Please hold your comments and questions. The second possible solution is that when and if Carlos Cryan makes the necessary moves to obtain title to the park, instead of doing nothing, we fight his claims. We would direct our legal advisor to argue that the town has had possession of the wall and land for at least 160 years, which is the time period we can prove through historic records. We can show the traditional and sentimental importance of the wall and park to hundreds and hundreds of citizens. This solution could result in a lengthy court battle which would cost many thousands of dollars in legal fees and necessitate raising funds. Citizens would have to share the expenses."

The crowd is mumbling as Darryl hands the microphone back to Mayor Angela Thayer. Ignoring the noise, she says, "Our third solution is to offer Carlos Cryan a deal. If he agrees to give up this claim, the town will deed to him an equal amount of property which is unused on the sunrise side of town. Admittedly, this land is undeveloped and has a morning view, but perhaps he would consider that he would avoid having large legal fees by settling. Also, his probable restaurant customers, the town's people, would be friends rather than enemies."

Mayor Thayer continues, "Our final solution is to wash our town's hands of controversy and build a new park and wall on the sunrise side of town. We would build a new wall together. We would invite all couples—young and old—to come and re-carve their initials in a concrete memorial. We would look forward rather than back!"

As Angela finishes, a long line of citizens appears to speak on the four proposals. The council secretary records their points of view, and a council member makes a video recording of the proceedings. For the most part, people are orderly, although it is clear they are angry with Carlos Cryan. Angela is not the only person there who is thinking that she would not want to be opening a restaurant after alienating most of the potential customers.

In the end, it seems most of the town's people are against the first and last solutions. They do not want to do nothing and hope a judge will rule against Carlos. They do not want to abandon their kissing wall, their traditions, and their sunset evenings in the park for a new park. The idea of romantic sunrises is only exciting to the most devoted morning people. It seems the town would be behind funding an attorney for the long haul or offering Cryan the alternate site and his neighbors' good will. Some people do say the surviving descendent of Keagan Cryan should have a piece of the town. So, Angela concludes the meeting by thanking everyone and stating that she and the council will go back to the drawing board and make more detailed proposals based on either fighting Cryan in court or offering him the sunrise land.

A few days later, Mayor Angela Thayer, Council President Darryl Jefferson, and the rest of the council meet to consider the two options favored by the citizens. They will either decide on fighting in court or trying to offer Carlos Cryan equal undeveloped land in Sunrise. The meeting goes well and they decide to offer Cryan land. They believe it is more positive and neighborly, and they leave the meeting feeling optimistic.

On the way home, Mayor Angela stops at the kissing wall to see the sunset. As usual, people are on park benches and blankets. Some are parked in cars to enjoy the spectacular colors of the sky. She is thinking that she hopes Cryan will accept their offer and leave these wonderful evenings for her town's residents to savor. She is wondering whether people enjoying this view have lower blood pressure! Then, she hears her husband's voice beside her and feels his hand in hers.

"Guess what?" Kevin says.

"What?" Angela responds.

Kevin continues, "Carlos Cryan discovered today that his great-great-great-great grandfather was Coogan Cryan, the brother of Keagan Cryan."

"What does that mean?" asks Angela with a puzzled look.

Kevin answers, "Well, Coogan Cryan didn't make it this far down the river. He settled a hundred and forty miles north of here and founded the town of Coogan Falls. So, Carlos Cryan is on his way there now to inform the people of Coogan Falls they owe him some riverfront property!"

Angela beams with joy, and then she hugs her husband. As they turn back toward the sunset, she thinks of all the evenings they have enjoyed at the kissing wall and feels relieved that the people of River Bend will be able to continue watching beautiful sunsets here.

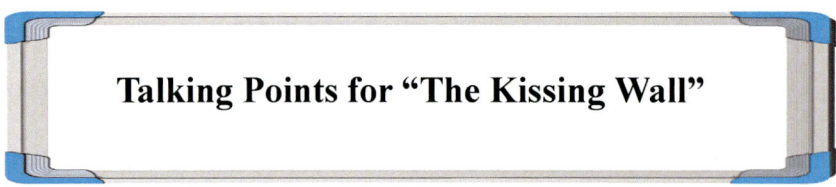

Talking Points for "The Kissing Wall"

- The town of "River Bend" is named for its location on the Ashland River.
- Two areas of the town are "Sunrise" and "Sunset."
- In the area of "Sunset" there is a beautiful park with a wall that people sit on to watch the sun as it goes down each day. The colors of the setting sun are awe-inspiring.
- The wall in the park is called "the kissing wall," because it is a romantic place.
- Angela and Kevin Thayer were engaged at the kissing wall, and Angela is now the town's mayor.
- A problem has arisen, because a town resident named Carlos Cryan is claiming that one of his ancestors founded the town. Carlos Cryan is claiming ownership of the kissing wall and the park where it stands.
- Mayor Angela Thayer and the town's council meet to discuss the problem. They devise four possible solutions.
- At a meeting with the town's people, Mayor Thayer and the town's council present the solutions, which are: (1) to do nothing and hope for the best; (2) to fight Carlos Cryan's claims in court; (3) to offer Carlos Cryan an equivalent amount of land on the "sunrise" side of town; or (4) to give Carlos the land he wants—along with the kissing wall—and build a new park and wall on the other side of town.
- In the end, and much to the relief of Mayor Thayer, none of the solutions is needed, because Carlos Cryan discovers that his ancestor did not found the town of River Bend.

COMPLEX STORIES

Hunting Treasure
by Virginia L. Smerglia

    This story is about a group of friends who get together every month for a fun activity. They are some couples and some singles, who began getting together as new neighbors in the wine country northeast of San Francisco. Their friendship has continued with a few moving out and newcomers joining. They have been together twenty years. For the most part, they like outdoor activities that are not too strenuous like boating, walking trails, biking, hiking, or even going to a football game. Each month, two group members plan their get-together, and they let the others know the arrangements, what they have to bring, and how to dress.

    So, it's early September and Anna and Greg are the planners for this month. They've thought of something really different—something they hope will be a success. It's a beautiful Saturday afternoon and about 70 degrees, with a crystal-clear blue sky: the blue that only northern California skies can be. The gardens in town are at their peak, and the vineyards surrounding the area are being harvested. It's what you might call a perfect, late summer day.

TELMIA

The group meets in the parking lot of the town diner. They observe that Anna and Greg have some mysterious-looking boxes—bigger than shoe boxes—piled in the back of Greg's van. When everyone has arrived, they gather to hear their instructions.

"Welcome, all!" says Anna. "Today, we've planned an adult treasure hunt. We're doing it in pairs so everyone who's a single should grab a partner."

Someone groans as the singles move around to find partners for the hunt. Finally, there are eight pairs. There are five married couples and three pairs of singles.

Greg continues, "Remember, keep an open mind! Your instructions are in the boxes Anna is handing out. Everyone has the same tasks on this treasure hunt, except you don't do them in the same order. So, no one has an advantage. When you have completed your hunt, please bring your box back to Anna's house where we'll be getting dinner ready on the deck. You have until five o'clock to finish the hunt. For most treasure hunts, the first one back wins. However, for this treasure hunt, whoever comes closest to answering the question wins."

Someone calls out, "What's the question?"

Anna answers, "Well, it's in your boxes, but the question is: 'What is the purpose of this treasure hunt?'"

Most pairs are pretty enthusiastic and begin reading their instructions. There are five identical tasks each pair must do. However, each couple must complete them in a different order. For one task the instruction reads: "Go to the college memory gardens. [There is a small private college in town.] Pick five flowers of different colors and a green fern. We have okayed this with the college, by the way. Arrange the flowers in the bottle of water found in your box. Put your arrangement in the Styrofoam® holder also found in your box."

A second task is to: "Go down 5th Street to the park on the river bank. Park your car and take the plastic bag in your box and walk down to the river. Find at least six river stones between the sizes of one- and six-inches-long and put them in your bag. Be sure you have stones of at least two colors."

Another task seems very strange, but the pairs plunge in nevertheless. The instructions say, "Drive up High Street until you are north of town. Keep going for two miles until you reach Scenic View Point. Get out of the car, take the spiral notebook and pen from your box, and sit together on one of the benches. Then, look out across the vineyards and hills. Now, together, write a poem that is four to ten lines."

A fourth instruction is to, "Drive down Collins Avenue to the old drug store. Take the five-dollar-bill from your treasure hunt box and go in. Buy the funniest, all-occasion greeting card that you can find. Remember, you both have to think that it's very funny!"

The instructions for the fifth task are: "Go South of High Street to Second Street and into the parking lot of St. Andrew's Episcopal Church. Take your spiral notebook and pen with you. Enter the front door and go into the sanctuary. Sit down in a pew. Don't worry! We have the priest's permission for you to enter the church. For a few minutes, look at the stained glass windows. Look at the beautiful sanctuary. Now, write down any observations the two of you have…just a few lines."

Needless to say, as the afternoon progresses, there is a lot of driving, a lot of thought, and quite a bit of laughter as the pairs complete their treasure hunt tasks. Of course, to win the game, they have to correctly guess Anna's and Greg's purpose in giving these five tasks. As a result, as each pair drives to Anna's house for their dinner together, there is a good bit of discussion.

By five o'clock all eight pairs have arrived on Anna's deck and are sipping wine and sodas, nibbling fruit and cheese, and sharing their funny greeting cards. They are tired, but anxious to hear each other's experiences and to find out the reason for this unusual treasure hunt. Anna asks each pair to place their flower arrangement into a long narrow basket she has put on the table. She also asks them to put their river rocks around the basket. Then, she lights candles. It is beautiful, as if a florist has come in and designed an arrangement. There are plenty of, "Ooh's" and "Ah's" at what they have randomly crafted together.

Greg says, "Do you want to find out if anyone guessed our purpose for this game now or wait until after we've eaten salad and pasta."

They all say, "Oh, now. Now!"

So, Greg and Anna go around the table asking each pair to say what they think the purpose of the treasure hunt is. Two pairs say they think it is to help everyone see the beauty of their town and the surrounding areas.

"Good guess," says Anna.

Three pairs say they think it is to give everyone a chance to relax and have fun at the end of a busy week."

"That's also a pretty good guess," Greg replies.

One pair say, "We thought it was about beauty and our area, but then we thought, 'Why did we have to buy the humorous greeting card?' So, we just had to say it was about experiencing lots of different emotions."

"That's deep," someone comments.

The last pair say, "We thought it was about expressing our creativity. We had to arrange flowers, write a poem, choose a funny card, and comment about something in Saint Andrew's, so we thought the purpose had to be to express our creativity."

Greg looks at Anna, smiles, and says, "Well that's pretty close. We wanted all of you dear friends to enjoy creating different types of things: flower arrangements, poems, observations of beauty but, most of all, we wanted you to feel and know that you are creative and talented individuals. To make that point, we'd like to read the poem written by one pair today as they travelled, hunted, and looked out over the vineyards and hills."

With that, Anna reads the following:
From the hills we saw green, growing rows.
And we knew that we are alive.

In a vineyard, twisting shoots entangled our feet.
And we laughed that we are friends.

Everywhere grapes' fragrances whispered.
And we recalled life's treasure: sharing moments.

Around our city rolled the hills, but sharply turned the roads.
And we felt life's journey: sometimes gentle, sometimes rough.

All day, above us dazzled the blue sky with flying birds.
And we remembered that our hearts can soar.

Talking Points for "Hunting Treasure"

- Anna and Greg gather each month with a group of friends.
- They all live in the same town northeast of San Francisco.
- Some in the group are couples, and some are single.
- Each month, two group members plan an activity, like hiking or boating.
- In September, Anna and Greg plan a treasure hunt with dinner to follow at Anna's house.
- Their treasure hunt is not for kids! There are a number of tasks, which include driving to a vineyard, going to a store, and writing a poem.
- The goal of the hunt is to figure out why they are doing it.
- At dinner that evening, Anna and Greg reveal that they want their friends to discover how talented and creative they are!
- From among their friends' poems, Anna gives a recitation of one that is lovely.

COMPLEX STORIES

Page 37

The Holidays Have Changed
by Virginia L. Smerglia

Karen was shopping for holiday gifts with her granddaughter, Christi. It was only the middle of November, but as we all know, the stores begin putting out Christmas decorations and gifts right after Halloween. Karen invited her granddaughter along because she was not yet old enough to drive, but she was old enough to want to do her own shopping. To be exact, Christi was fourteen. Karen was happy that Christi still liked to do things with her and that they always had fun being together.

After they had shopped for three hours, Karen said, "Christi, I think it's time for lunch. Are you hungry?"

"Grandma, I am starved and I see a nice restaurant right across the street. I think they have great burgers and salads," Christi responded.

So Karen and Christi went into the restaurant and got a table by the window where they could watch other shoppers and enjoy the quiet. Karen felt good that Christi had gotten very nice gifts for her mom and dad and brothers. It was hard to find something on a teenager's budget. After they ordered lunch, they talked about all the holiday fun that was coming: six weeks of festivities if you counted from the week before Thanksgiving until New Year's Day.

Christi asked, "What kinds of things did you do when you were my age, Grandma? Were the celebrations mostly the same as we have now?"

Karen explained, "Oh, Christi, things were very different! First of all, the stores didn't put out their decorations until the weekend after Thanksgiving, at least. And, no one thought of putting up decorations in their houses until the week before Christmas!"

Astonished, Christi exclaimed, "The week before Christmas? How could that be fun, Grandma? You would only have the holidays for two weeks!"

Karen answered, "Well, it was just so much fun, Christi! First of all, everyone had a real Christmas tree and they couldn't last in the house for five or six weeks. Even in two weeks, they would start to lose their needles and, by New Year's Eve, my parents were afraid to leave the tree lights on for very long in case it was a fire hazard."

"So, first, we would be finished with school. On the last day before holiday vacation when I was in elementary school, we would all go to the auditorium after lunch. The principal would lead us in singing songs like, "Up On The Housetop" and "Here Comes Santa Claus." Then we'd do "Jingle Bells" and "Away In A Manger." Then, we'd be dismissed to our classes where the room mothers would have homemade frosted cutout cookies of Santa and angels and stars. We'd have cookies and little cups of ice cream and talk about what we hoped to get for Christmas gifts. When I went

COMPLEX STORIES

home from school on that last day before the holidays, I was on top of the world! I knew we would go the next day to pick out our Christmas tree."

Smiling and in awe, Christi asked, "Did your family cut down your own tree, Grandma?"

Karen replied, "No, Christi, we didn't really live in the country and we bought our tree every year from the same place. So, it was a matter of walking around the tree lot and deciding. My parents always liked long-needled trees rather than the short-needled spruce trees. And, when we finally got the tree home, it was quite a production to put it up. My daddy, your great-grandfather, would decide whether it looked even."

"Even?" said Christi.

Karen went on, "You know, with no big bare spots where there were no branches. Sometimes, he would saw off a branch from one side and then drill a hole in the other side and move the branch. Or, he would decide to turn and turn the tree before he was satisfied which was the best side and that would be the side toward the living room, away from the window. Some years, he would wire the tree to the wall or a window if it seemed crooked."

"It seems like a lot of work," Christi said. "So, what happened next?"

Karen continued, "Well, we had to put it in water, of course. Then, my father would start the lights. He was very picky about those. My brother and I would usually get bored and find something else to do because we knew it would be a long time before our dad got the lights on to his satisfaction so we could start putting on the ornaments. The lights had to be even, you know!"

"Grandma, it seems like your dad was pretty up-tight about everything being even!" Christi remarked.

Karen responded, "That he was! And, there's more! After we had the ornaments on the tree, we would put thin metallic icicles on every branch. I don't even know if the stores still have them. They were long strands. Every year, we had to put them on one-by-one and it took forever! One year, we visited our aunt and uncle in Buffalo. They were very wealthy and their tree was decorated by professional florists. It was twelve feet tall and had huge gold balls on it and big gobs of the same kinds of silver icicles that we had, but they looked like someone stood back and threw thousands of them on the tree. My brother and I were waiting for our parents to roll their eyes, because my father never would have allowed such a thing. And, here our aunt and uncle had paid to have people make this mess."

Christi was amazed and asked, "So, what did your parents say, Grandma?"

Karen answered, "Well this uncle was my mother's brother and she loved him dearly. She stood there and said, 'My, what a wonderful, lovely tree you have!' My dad didn't say a word, of course, but we knew what he was thinking. And, when we got back home the next day, he just looked at our tree and said, 'I think I prefer this way of doing the icicles, Doris!' That was my mom's name, as you know."

"Was that the end of decorating for Christmas, Grandma?" Christi inquired.

Karen's response was: "No, there is one more important thing, Christi. You haven't heard me say much about my mother in all of this. That is because her specialty was making a winter village under the tree. She would lay down rolls of white cotton. Then, she would take dark sand and make roads and place all of her little houses on the roads to make neighborhoods. She had a church, too. Then, she would cut a piece out of the cotton and put a mirror under it for an ice pond. She had made people, believe it or not, out of construction paper. She had ice skaters with stocking caps and mittens. Carefully, she would position them on the mirror, so that they appeared to be skating on ice. She even made a sliding board and teeter-totter and had a playground and little metal cars for the roads. Finally, there were two more things, very special touches which my brother and I waited for."

"What were they, Grandma?" Christi begged.

Karen's eyes sparkled to see how intrigued her granddaughter was. Then, she explained, "Well, she had a Santa on skis. She would place him where the white cotton covered the tree stand, so it looked like he was skiing down a hill into the village with his backpack of toys. Then, she would take salt and dye it blue with food coloring. She would need almost a whole box of table salt. As you know, we lived by Lake Erie when I was growing up, Christi. So, on the cotton behind the tree, she would sprinkle the salt so that it looked like the village was on the edge of a big lake. She wanted to make it seem like our town, on the shore of Lake Erie."

Bringing them out of the past and into their present lunch and shopping trip, Karen exclaimed, "Oh dear, my sweet girl, you must be very bored with your Grandma's long story. Our lunch is all done and I know you want to get back to our shopping."

Christi touched Karen's hand across the lunch table and said, "Grandma, when you tell me stories of how your life was growing up, it makes me feel like we're both the same age just for a little while. I like to think of you at fourteen and what it must have been like back then. Thank you for sharing your Christmas memories with me. Now, let's get back to shopping. We have to find a present for Grandpa!"

Talking Points for "The Holidays Have Changed"

- Karen went Christmas shopping with her fourteen-year-old granddaughter, Christi.
- Although she wasn't old enough to drive yet, Christi wanted to buy Christmas presents for family members.
- Midway through their shopping trip, Karen and Christi stopped for lunch at a restaurant.
- During lunch, Karen told Christi about her childhood Christmas traditions, like decorating the tree.
- When Karen was a child, most people had real trees as Christmas trees, and most people's decorations were displayed for only two weeks.
- Karen explained that her father was very particular about the Christmas tree and its decorations—including "evening out" the tree's branches and placing silver icicles on it.
- Karen also told Christi about a trip to her aunt's and uncle's house. They had a professionally decorated Christmas tree, but it wasn't as nicely done as the one Karen's parents had put up.
- Karen reminisced about her mother's special Christmas village under the tree. It had a pond, Santa on skis, and a lake!
- Christi enjoyed hearing about her grandmother's childhood Christmas traditions.

Home From Paris
by Lauren Smerglia Seifert

For many people in Europe, August is called "holiday." You might as well say that "Everyone is on vacation!" For Carrie Chapman, August is very special this year, because her daughter is coming home "on holiday" from Paris.

Carrie is an accountant in Evansville, Indiana. Her daughter, Nora Elizabeth, is studying interior design in Paris, and she has been there for a year. In Evansville, where Carrie raised Nora, life is Midwestern. Some people call Evansville, "River City" because it rests in a lush and fertile region of the Ohio River Valley. Most people make a living at businesses in town, in manufacturing and distribution, at one of the two universities, or by farming in the surrounding areas.

Carrie attended the University of Evansville and received a degree in accounting. Then, she started working for a local firm. She thought Nora might do something similar, but Nora Elizabeth was always drawn to the arts, music, fashion, and design. When one of her high school art teachers suggested interior design and decorating, Nora was enraptured. She applied to numerous programs abroad and was accepted to two of them. It had been hard for Carrie to wave good-bye to her only child at the airport as she watched the eighteen-year-old head off to the college of her choosing—in Paris. However, she wouldn't have stopped her. Carrie wanted her daughter to have her dreams fulfilled!

Now, it was August 1st, and Nora would be home in two days. Carrie couldn't wait to see her, but she worked diligently to keep her attention on tasks at the office. At lunchtime, she was on her way to meet a friend at a local restaurant, when her boss stopped her.

"Carrie, do you have a second?" he asked.

A bit flustered and wondering whether she would be leaving her friend waiting, Carrie replied, "Sure, Frank. What's up?"

"Listen," Frank said. "I'm in a bit of a pickle, and I have a favor to ask. I'm sure you're aware that my assistant is out on maternity leave, right?" Carrie nodded, and Frank continued, "Well, she usually helps me to put together dinners for clients. Before she went on leave, she worked to set up a number of special occasions for me, so that I could continue to entertain important clients while she was gone. Well, something has come up unexpectedly. I have one of our firm's most important customers coming here from New York City in just a week. I need help, and I just didn't know who else to ask. I realize that this isn't part of your job description as an accountant, but I would be very grateful if you would help me arrange a gathering."

Carrie was quiet as she thought about her daughter's arrival from Paris. Ugh!

This gathering would happen right in the middle of their vacation together before Nora had to return to France. However, when Carrie looked at Frank's worried expression, she just couldn't say "no." So she replied, "Frank, don't worry. If it's okay with you, I can start making arrangements as soon as I return from lunch today."

With a look of relief, Frank thanked Carrie for her help. Then, she went off to meet her friend for lunch. Back at the office after lunch, Carrie collected her boss' notes about the clients who would be attending the gathering in a week's time. Of all things, they were interior designers! They would be arriving in Evansville in seven days, and Frank wanted to treat them to a catered dinner, so Carrie called around to find a caterer and a hall in which to hold the event. She was very fortunate to find both, and had the whole dinner planned within two business days.

When August 3rd arrived—bringing Nora with it—Carrie's mind turned toward home, and she let her boss' dinner slip from her mind. Everything appeared to be in order, and she believed that the dinner plans were adequately made. Picking Nora up from the airport, Carrie talked the whole way home: catching her daughter up on all the "River City" news. When they got home, they stayed up most of the night gabbing and laughing.

Nora said, "Oh, Mom! I've missed you so much! And I've missed our all-night conversations about everything under the sun!"

"Me, too, Honey," Carrie responded, hugging her daughter and holding her tightly. She didn't want to let her go, because she loved those "Nora hugs."

"I suppose we ought to get to bed, right? I'm sure that we'll have more to talk about when the sun comes up again," Nora suggested, as she yawned—exhausted from the plane ride and the long day.

For the next five days, Carrie thought very little about work. She was on vacation, and she was enjoying having her girl home! They visited the nearby Angel Mounds—which were long ago inhabited by a large population of Native Americans who are referred to as "Mississippian." Since Nora was a small child, she and Carrie enjoyed their trips to the mounds—where they would talk about what it must have been like to live on this land so long ago.

The two also stayed home and just enjoyed each other's company. Carrie loved hearing about Nora's classes and activities in interior design. They were so very different than her own experiences in college as an accounting major! Nora described various projects on which she had been working: helping one of her professors to decorate the foyer of a grand Parisian hotel, working with classmates on a miniature-sized model of The Palace at Versailles, and lending her talents to an internship at a Parisian design firm. It sounded so exciting!

The time went quickly, and it was now August 8th: the day when Carrie's boss would entertain clients from New York City. She had promised that she would go to the banquet hall and check to be sure that everything was ready for the event. She mentioned it to her daughter, and Nora offered to go with her to check the venue and talk to the caterer.

When they arrived at the hall, everything outside looked good. The shrubberies were nicely trimmed, the flowers were blooming, and the parking lot had just been resealed. It was pleasing to the eye. As they entered through the front doors of the banquet hall, Nora remarked that she had whiffed the odors of scrumptious food. She said, "Mom, I smell something delicious. That's a very good sign!"

Then, the two women entered the hall where the dinner would take place, and Carrie's heart sank. Bright fluorescent lights, white tablecloths on three round tables, and plain white metal chairs. There were no centerpieces. There was no décor. Oh, dear! Her boss would be entertaining one of the firm's most important clients—who just happened to be interior designers—and the banquet hall was plain, bland, plain!

Carrie gasped and looked at her daughter. Together, they searched for the banquet hall's manager and were told that she had gone home sick that day: leaving instructions for plain white linens with no decorations in the main dining room.

With a moan, Carrie said, "Oh, dear. This is a disaster. Frank cannot entertain internationally known interior designers from New York City in a room like this!" Turning to her daughter, Carrie said, "Honey, I'm in over my head here. Can you help?"

If there was one thing that Nora Elizabeth Chapman wanted to do in her life, it was to help her mom and show her that all the money she was shelling out for college was going to good use. Now, she had the opportunity! She asked, "Mom, how much time do we have?"

"Two hours and forty-five minutes," responded Carrie, her voice quivering nervously.

"Mom, we are superwomen. We can do this! All this room needs is a bit of PAHS-MON-TREE!" Nora urged happily—ending her utterance in the French that she was so accustomed to speaking each day in Paris.

"It needs what?" Carrie quizzed.

Her daughter laughed with sparkling eyes and said, "It's spelled P-A-S-S-E-M-E-N-T-E-R-I-E, and it's pronounced PAHS-MON-TREE—like a type of tree that someone's pa would own." Then, she giggled, continuing, "Isn't it a funny word, Mom? PAHS-MON-TREE! It is one of the first words I learned in design school. It means, 'trimmings' or 'decoration.'"

Carrie smiled and took her daughter's arm. Then, she replied, "It is a funny word. Let's go find some PAHS-MON-TREE for this room, so that I won't get fired!"

Nora drove. It was a refreshing change from riding the Parisian "Metro"—which is the French subway. Carrie and Nora went to a fabric store, a consignment shop, and a discount store. They had less than three hours to find everything they would need and return to decorate. It was quite a challenge, but Nora had good ideas from the start. Because it was August, the theme would be sunshine and summertime. In her mind's eye, she pictured a sunflower bathed in bright sunlight. She would use those colors: of the yellow petals and the green stem. However, it must be tastefully done, and they would have to make use of the white linens that the banquet hall manager had already set out. Nora's idea was to use a refreshing, yellow fabric overlay on each table. The yellow pieces would lay on top of the white linen. Also, Nora would have to hunt for something green to create an allusion to the verdant green of late summer. When she explained the idea to her mother, Carrie loved it.

"It sounds perfect!" Carrie exclaimed.

At the discount store, Nora and Carrie found square tablecloths of pale yellow lace, so they purchased three of them: one for each table. In addition, there were beautiful, pillar-style candles in deep green. They would be stunning against the background of yellow lace on white linen.

After the discount store, Nora and Carrie went to a fabric shop to buy trim: the type with little pompons dangling from it. Nora's idea was to purchase several yards of this trim in vibrant yellow-gold, snip the pompons off, and sprinkle them around the center of each table. At the consignment shop, the two women found three lovely glass candle holders. They were tall pedestals on which a pillar candle could be set. These would work well as part of the centerpieces!

Rushing back to the banquet hall, Carrie and Nora had just forty minutes to decorate. Carefully, they laid the yellow lace over the white linen on each of the round tables. Then, they placed a glass pedestal in the center of each one. Next, Carrie unwrapped the deep green pillar candles and positioned them on the glass pedestals. Finally, using a pair of scissors they had borrowed from the caterers—who were bustling around back in the kitchen—Nora snipped the pompons from the gold trim she had bought. She sprinkled them around generously so that the pompons looked like seed pods or small pieces of fruit which had landed in such a way as to surround the bases of the glass pedestals. After she returned the scissors to the caterer, Nora walked back into the banquet hall to find her mom beaming.

"Oh, Nora! It is just perfect! The bright yellow with crystal and green—against the white linen is lovely. I only wish that we could do something about these ghastly white metal chairs. They are atrocious!" Carrie exclaimed.

"Not to worry, Mom!" Nora replied, and with that, she pulled out 24 very long table runners that matched the yellow lace on the tables. She had seen them in packages of 12 at the discount store. Now, she was glad that she had bought two packages.

Quickly, Nora draped a table runner over the back of each chair. As she was doing this, she asked her mom to seek a stapler from someone in the banquet hall's office. When Carrie returned with the stapler, Nora rapidly pulled the two sides of a table runner under each chair's back and stapled it beneath with a little piece of the pompon trim, so that two gold pompons hung down and the trim covered the staple.

    Carrie stared at the backs of the chairs as her daughter raced around the room—adorning each ugly metal chair with its own yellow lace and pompons. She clapped and said, "Bravo! Bravo! Nora the chairs look amazing. Who knew that they were just white metal chairs ten minutes ago?"

    As mother and daughter turned to leave, having satisfied themselves that the ugly, plain banquet room was now ready for an evening dinner with important clients, Carrie's boss entered. He had already spoken with the caterer about dinner. Now, he gazed around the room—blinking. Then, he said, "Wow! Carrie the room looks great. Thank you so much for helping me with this event."

    Carrie grinned and responded, "You're welcome, Frank. I'll take credit for booking the caterer and the banquet hall, but you'll have to give credit to my daughter Nora for all the PAHS-MON-TREE! She is currently working on a bachelor's degree in interior design, and apparently, she has learned all about 'brick-a-brack' and 'trimmings.'"

    Knowing that her boss was satisfied, Carrie began to walk out of the room with her daughter. She and Nora had worn dresses, because they planned to have a girl's night out at a fancy restaurant after they checked the banquet hall for Frank. As they exited, Frank called after them, "Hey! Are you two doing anything this evening? Perhaps, you'd like to join us? Maybe Nora could help me as I try to engage our clients in conversation about their passion for interior design. After all, what do I know about it? I'm just their accountant."

    With that, Carrie and Nora were invited to join in the evening of entertaining the accounting firm's clients. It was a lovely dinner, and the clients loved Nora's idea of sprinkling golden pompons over yellow lace on each table. They were even more impressed when they discovered that Nora was just eighteen and in her first year studying interior design. The best news of all is that this is the story about how Nora met people who own an interior design firm in New York City. They just happen to be the same people who offered her a job as soon as she finished college!

COMPLEX STORIES

Talking Points for "Home From Paris"

- Carrie Chapman is an accountant in Evansville, Indiana.
- She has a daughter named Nora Elizabeth, who is studying interior design in Paris.
- Nora made plans to come home for a "holiday" during August, and Carrie couldn't wait to see her girl!
- Evansville is a very nice place to live: with manufacturing and distribution; local businesses; and farming in this lush area in the Ohio River Valley.
- Just a few days before Nora was due home, Carrie's boss asked her to help him plan an event. His assistant was out on maternity leave and he needed to entertain important clients, who are interior designers.
- Carrie agreed to help, and by the time her daughter had arrived home from Paris, Carrie believed that she had adequately arranged for catering and the banquet hall for her boss.
- Carrie and Nora spent a lovely week of vacation. They gabbed a lot, and they visited the Angel Mounds—one of their favorite historic sites.
- On the day of her boss' big dinner, Carrie decided that she should go to the banquet hall in order to make sure that everything was ready for the evening. Nora decided to go with her mother.
- When they arrived at the banquet hall, the two women were shocked that the room looked awful: with plain white linens and ugly white metal chairs.
- Nora helped her mom, as they rushed around from store to store finding "PAHS-MON-TREE" (a French word, "passementerie," meaning "trimmings" or "décor") for the banquet room.
- Nora's arrangement of refreshing yellow lace over the white linens turned out beautifully. In the center of each table, she placed a glass pedestal with a dark green candle on it. Then, she sprinkled little yellow-gold pompons around the base of each pedestal. Finally, she covered the backs of the ugly metal chairs with long, yellow lace table runners—securing them with staples and a bit of the pompon trim.
- Carrie's boss, Frank, was so impressed with the ladies' decorations that he asked them to stay and help him entertain the interior designers.
- They did, and this is how Nora Elizabeth Chapman secured her first job. The interior designers were so impressed with her that they ended up hiring her after she finished college!
- For more about Evansville, visit **http://www.evansvillegov.org/** or use a search engine, like Google® to find out about the "River City" in Indiana.

A Hard, Hard Question
by Virginia L. Smerglia

This is a story about two friends, Ben and Gloria. They worked together in the same office for more than thirty years. Now, Ben and Gloria are both retired and they are also both widowed. They enjoy each other's company and usually manage to spend some time together every week. Their relationship is not about romance; it is a friendship. They like many of the same things, such as trying new restaurants for lunch or dinner. Sometimes, they go to a movie or a concert. In warm weather, they may go for a walk or even a hike.

Because they worked together for so many years, Ben and Gloria know each other's personalities pretty well. They've always gotten along, and they know a lot about each other's lives. For example, Ben knows that Gloria worked very hard at her job and that at least twice she was passed over for promotions she deserved. He also knows that she was never bitter about it. Ben also sees that Gloria is quite proud of her daughter who is an attorney and that she worries about her son who can't seem to keep a job. Gloria is aware of Ben's loneliness and that he still misses his wife very much—even though it is ten years since she passed away. She knows that he is a kind person and that he had a reputation of being a very fair manager in his department at work. In addition to knowing each other well, Ben and Gloria also respect and trust each other. That's probably why their friendship is so valuable to them.

One summer day, they tried a new restaurant for lunch and decided to go on some walking trails in the park after lunch. They were walking along when Gloria said, "Can I ask you a question?"

Ben looked surprised and said, "Of course you may!"

Gloria said, "Well, I'll warn you that this question might be hard to answer."

"Okay, go for it," Ben replied.

So, Gloria asked, "Ben, if you could change one thing you did in your life, what would it be?"

Ben stopped walking and looked out over a stream and meadow they were passing. "Wow, Gloria! Let me think," he responded.

They walked on and he was quiet for a few minutes. When she looked over at him, Gloria saw that Ben had a tear in his eye. He removed a white handkerchief from his pocket, unfolded it, removed his glasses, and wiped his eyes slowly while he pondered Gloria's difficult question.

"If I could change something, it would be the way I treated my parents when I was in college," he said. "My parents had a shoe store and they worked very hard. Their dream was for me to go to college, which neither of them had been able to do. They managed to save enough money so I could go away to school. They sent me to a very good school and I didn't even have to work. I was able to put my time into studying and also having some fun."

Ben continued, "While I was at school, I also took on the attitude that having a college education would somehow make me better than other people. In other words, I got a big head. [Gloria laughed at that.] When I came home for the holidays my freshman year, my parents were so excited. They were proud of me and anxious to hear about my classes and the details of my college life. I was happy to see them, but my new attitude also included looking down on my own parents, because they hadn't gone to college. I was pretty arrogant and selfish the whole time I was home."

"One evening, Mom was asking about what I was studying in my classes. I purposely talked about my psychology and geology classes using the terms I knew she wouldn't understand. I was showing off big-time. I could just as easily have talked about what I was learning in everyday language. My mother was not a stupid person; she would have been delighted to hear new ideas. However, I wanted to show how important and smart I was. I saw the look on her face. She was embarrassed not to understand what I was talking about. She didn't ask about my classes again after that."

"I made my parents feel uneducated and ignorant. Worse, I'm sure they felt we would no longer be as close, because they would be boring to me now. I can still see my mom's face and the loss and embarrassment she was feeling. I have never forgiven myself for hurting them on purpose. If I could go back to that time and show them my appreciation for their hard work and the privileges it gave me, that would be the most important thing to change in my life."

As Ben folded his handkerchief and put it back into his pocket, Gloria touched his arm. She asked, "Did you ever tell them later how much you appreciated them?"

"Yes, but somehow it doesn't erase the pain I caused them, because that first sharing of what I was doing and learning was spoiled for them and I humiliated them," he said solemnly.

Then, Gloria asked, "Ben, did you have a good relationship with them later? Did they share in your family's life? Did you spend time with them?"

"Yes, to all of those questions," he answered.

"Well, then, you did erase those bad memories for them. Young people are trying to figure out how the world works, and they often say and do things that don't make much sense later. Most of us do things when we're young that make our parents wonder whether the values they taught us have disappeared! I remember one pastor I had used to say, 'At twenty-five, I was amazed at how much my parents had learned since I was eighteen.'" Ben chuckled, and Gloria went on, "I'll bet your parents knew that you were testing the waters with your new knowledge."

TELMIA

Gloria took Ben's hand in hers as they walked on. After they were quiet for awhile, Ben said, "Thanks, Gloria! You've made me feel better about something that has been bothering me for forty years! So, now, let me ask you, 'What one thing would you change in your past if you had the chance?'"

Gloria was quiet for a minute. Then, she said, "We're going to need some ice cream if you're going to hear my story."

Ben smiled and responded, "Let's go. I'm ready for both!"

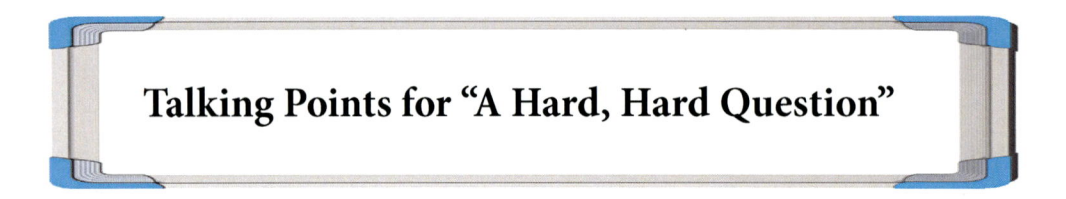

Talking Points for "A Hard, Hard Question"

- Ben and Gloria are widowed and have been friends for more than thirty years.
- They worked at the same company and are now, both, retired.
- Just friends, Ben and Gloria enjoy spending time together. They take walks, go to restaurants, and have a lot to talk about.
- One day, while they were walking in a beautiful park, Gloria asked Ben a difficult question: "If he could change one thing in his life, what would he have done differently?"
- Ben told Gloria about his first year in college, when he came home to visit.
- He used lots of big words and technical terms to show off and so that his mother wouldn't understand what he was saying. He has very deep regrets about it.
- Gloria consoled him—pointing out that the things he did later showed them that he didn't look down on his parents and that he was very grateful that they had provided a way for him to go to college.
- After that, Ben turned the tables and asked Gloria the same hard question.
- She suggested that they get some ice cream, because hers was going to be a long story to tell!

Page 50

COMPLEX STORIES

Cross That Bridge When You Come To It
by Virginia L. Smerglia

    In San Francisco's Chinatown lives a Chinese family. They are a large and happy family who own a restaurant. The family's name is Linn and their restaurant is called Linn Food. In Chinatown, which is very crowded, many businesses and restaurants are sandwiched into very small areas. Some are downstairs. To dine at Linn Food, customers have to go down a set of stairs from the street. Most people don't mind, because the food there is very delicious. It has been delicious for three generations of the Linn family.

TELMIA

Mama and Papa Linn started this family restaurant, and they are both in their eighties now. They have a son and a daughter who are middle-aged—Carol and Louis—who now do most of the work of running the restaurant. Mama and Papa are proud to have five grandchildren from the ages of fourteen to twenty-one who also work at Linn Food. If you stop someone who lives in Chinatown and ask where to get a good meal, it is likely you will be told to go downstairs to Linn Food.

Even though they are getting older, Mama and Papa Linn still work in the restaurant. They are happy because they do the jobs they like. No more washing dishes and taking garbage out for them! Mama loves preparing the soups. She loves cutting the vegetables by hand and she really loves making wontons, which look like little ravioli's, for the wonton soup.

Papa loves talking with the customers. He has always enjoyed talking with everyone, whether they are people he sees every day from the neighborhood or tourists from across the country or even from other countries. He sometimes sits down for a few minutes with customers to find out how things are going for them. He loves asking tourists about their hometowns. Of course, he also asks how they like their meals and whether they need anything. Papa's smiling eyes and courtesy always help business!

Linn Food seems to do well through good and bad economic times. It still supports this large family. They all work well together and appreciate their customers. Mama and Papa brought courtesy with them from their Chinese culture. The children and grandchildren have learned the secret recipes that Mama and Papa got from their parents and grandparents. The grandchildren have also learned the importance of courtesy and kindness.

Soon, Mama and Papa will be celebrating their fifty-fifth wedding anniversary. Their family is thinking of closing the restaurant for a weekend and having a big party for them. Their daughter, Carol, has discovered her parents have a secret wish. They want to walk across the Golden Gate Bridge! That's right: WALK across the Golden Gate Bridge. Why? Well, they have been very busy running the restaurant and raising children. Over the years, they learned to speak English, they had to learn business laws, and they had to work "twenty-four-seven," as people say now.

They have scarcely ever been out of Chinatown. They have never been across the Golden Gate Bridge to see what's on the other side. Now, they want to walk across the bridge and then to the park on the other side and look back at their city!

Carol says, "Mama, Papa, it's a very long walk, the better part of two miles!"

"We know that," says Papa, "but we walk around all day. Can it be further than we walk in a day?"

Carol can't argue with that. So, she asks, "What if it's raining on your anniversary?"

"We'll carry umbrellas," says Mama. "But, you know, Carol, it almost never rains in San Francisco in August!"

Carol talks with her brother, Louis, and they agree. Their parents should be able to do anything they want to on their fifty-fifth wedding anniversary. They make a plan with the grandchildren. The whole family is fourteen people. They will all walk across the bridge with Mama and Papa. They will go to the scenic viewing area on the other side and take Mama and Papa's picture with the city behind them. Louis has a friend who runs an airport shuttle company. He will see if the friend can drive the whole family back across the Golden Gate Bridge for a party at the restaurant. First they will walk across the bridge. Then, they will have their picture taken, and after that, they will drive back to the restaurant for the anniversary party. It should be an exciting day!

The plans are made and August 15th dawns beautiful and sunny, with no San Francisco fog!! The walk across the bridge is planned for three o'clock in the afternoon. Mama and Papa have agreed to be driven from the restaurant to the bridge. So, Louis' friend sends the shuttle at 2:45 P.M. and the whole family, including Mama and Papa, piles in. At the sidewalk that crosses the Golden Gate Bridge, all fourteen of them get out. Then a surprise: A reporter from one of the television stations is there waiting with a photographer. They've heard about this walk and they want to take a picture of Mama and Papa and their entire family for the weekend news shows.

Everyone is surprised except Louis! H-m-m-m. Mama and Papa are shy, but the reporter wants to know about their restaurant and how many years they have been serving food in Chinatown. Then, the photographer snaps some pictures and winks at Louis.

Mama is excited to begin the walk. She looks out at the ocean as the group starts walking. "Oh, look, Papa!" she says.

They see a couple of ships coming from the Pacific Ocean into the bay. As they travel across the bridge, they look up at the beautiful towering red-orange spans of the wondrous bridge. Their children and grandchildren begin to realize this is not just a little anniversary dream, but a special experience for all of them.

COMPLEX STORIES

When they are about two-thirds of the way across the bridge, Papa looks back and sees the city skyline. The buildings shine in the afternoon sun. Beautiful! Then, as he turns toward the view across the bay, he sees the water sparkling like diamonds as he looks toward Oakland and San Rafael on the opposite side. Then, he sees the beautiful wooded hills of Marin County at the end of the bridge. Tears spring to his eyes. "It's almost too much for one person to take in," he says. He holds Mama's hand as they turn slowly and take in each view. Louis takes pictures so they can enjoy the views again and again.

Finally, the group reaches the northern side of the Golden Gate Bridge in Marin County. The shuttle picks them up and drives them into the scenic view parking area. Louis and Carol scurry to the back of the shuttle where they have stowed a cooler with champagne, strawberries, and cheese.

"Wait!" says Louis. "Everyone gets champagne and a little box of strawberries and cheese."

The group is happy to sit for a few minutes after their long walk and to have some refreshment. Carol has arranged to have music playing on the shuttle bus' sound system. It's Vivaldi's "Four Seasons," one of her parents' favorites. The beautiful stringed instruments along with the sun on the San Francisco skyline and the champagne and strawberries make this an exceptional day.

After all are served, Carol says, "Mama, Papa, we are so honored to be your children. You teach all of us, each day, about true happiness…sharing life's moments no matter what they bring, enjoying each other, learning from the happenings of every day together. Happy fifty-fifth wedding anniversary!"

The whole family stands and cheers. Everybody hugs! As they step off the bus to get their picture taken with their city in the background, Papa says, "Oh, thank you, Carol! Thank you, Louis! Thank you, everyone! Look at our city! I love seeing our city from this side of the Golden Gate Bridge! I love our city!"

Mama says, "I love this day!!"

Talking Points for "Cross That Bridge When You Come To It"

- Mama and Papa Linn live in Chinatown in San Francisco.
- When they came to the U.S. from China, they opened a restaurant.
- Two generations later, the whole Linn Family works in the restaurant.
- Mama and Papa will celebrate their fifty-fifth wedding anniversary, and their children—Carol and Louis—want to have a special celebration.
- Mama Linn has always wanted to walk across the Golden Gate Bridge. So, the whole family will walk across the bridge together.
- August 15th is sunny and bright. It is the day of the big event!
- When they arrive at the Golden Gate Bridge by shuttle bus, a reporter is waiting to take their photo.
- The whole family walks across the Golden Gate Bridge.
- Then, they enjoy champagne, cheese, and strawberries as they ride back across the Bridge.
- Mama and Papa love each other, their family, and their city.

COMPLEX STORIES

The Mailman's Mystery
by Virginia L. Smerglia

    This story takes place in downtown Cleveland. It is about a mailman named Wilson and some mysterious events which occurred on his mail route. As Wilson will tell you, he likes to be called a "postal carrier" or a "mail carrier."

    As you can imagine, since his route is in downtown Cleveland, most of his customers are in business offices. He delivers mail to the offices of doctors, dentists, lawyers, accountants, financial advisors, and even some companies. Many people know him because he goes into the offices with his big mail sacks and he is usually met by the workers assigned to receive the mail. Wilson's route is actually only one building. Because it has forty-five floors and many offices on each floor, it takes Wilson all day to deliver to the offices in that building. He has a cart to transport the mail bags, and he uses the service elevators to move it from floor to floor.

TELMIA

One sunny Tuesday morning in June, Wilson was in high spirits as he started his mail deliveries, because he and his brother were going to see the Cleveland Indians play that night. He was imagining those great stadium hotdogs, some cold beer, popcorn, and perfect weather. His favorite pitcher was on the mound that night and he wanted to be sure to be there for the first pitch. He was making good time going in and out of offices and greeting everyone with a smile. Wilson was telling people he knew well that he was going to the game. When he got to the ninth floor, he left his cart in the hall and carried the heavy sack into a doctor's office. He stopped to chitchat with Carol, the receptionist, because he knew she was an Indians fan.

When Wilson came out into the hall and started to move his cart, there on top of his sacks of mail sat a monkey. That's right! Wilson saw a very little monkey sitting on top of his mail cart. Wilson looked in disbelief. What was a monkey doing on his cart? How would a monkey get into a building in the middle of downtown Cleveland? He thought of the zoo, but the zoo was several miles away on the other side of the Cuyahoga River. He went back into the doctor's office and asked Carol if she knew anything about someone on that floor having a pet monkey.

Page 58

She said, "We'd better call the security guards downstairs, but first I want to see it. Is it cute?"

Wilson and Carol walked back out to his cart in the hallway, but [surprise!] there was no monkey! Carol thought maybe Wilson was playing a joke on her, but he assured her that the monkey was real. It had been sitting there, blinking its eyes at him and moving around on top of his mail cart. They walked down the hall and stopped in a few other offices but saw no monkey. So, Wilson went into Carol's office and called the security guards. He described the monkey's size and color. It was strange, but Wilson couldn't stay on the ninth floor any longer. He had to go on with his deliveries.

After work, Wilson went home, changed, met his brother at the stadium, and watched an exciting baseball game. The Indians won by one run in the ninth inning! It was a warm summer evening. There was lots of good food to eat, and Wilson did not think about the little monkey again.

The next day, Wilson went about his mail delivery route as usual. When he got to the ninth floor, he looked around for the monkey but did not see anything. He talked to Carol about the Indians' exciting win. As he left, Wilson asked her if there was any news about the monkey.

Carol answered, "No. Security searched, but they found nothing."

Wilson continued his delivery route. When he came back to his cart from an office on the twelfth floor—[guess what?]—there again was the monkey sitting as pretty as you please on top of his mail cart. This time, the monkey was eating an oatmeal cookie!

Taking no chances, Wilson pulled out his cell phone and dialed security. In a few minutes, two elevators opened at the same time and as the security guards exited from one elevator, the monkey jumped onto the other—which was empty—and the doors closed. The guards tried to catch the monkey as they came out of the elevator, but it was just too fast!

Now, there was a mystery, and there was a little monkey loose in the office building! The guards asked Wilson if he had any idea why the monkey kept going to his mail cart, in particular. He didn't know why and he was anxious to get to the rest of his rounds, because he had lost so much time over the monkey.

Needless to say, on the next day, which was Thursday, Wilson was nervous and wondering whether the monkey would reappear. He had told his family and some of his friends about the animal. None of them knew anyone with a pet monkey. Wilson was relieved when Thursday came and went with no more sightings of the monkey and, by the end of the day, Wilson figured the monkey had gone back to wherever he was from.

Friday morning dawned hot and humid in Cleveland. It was predicted to be 96 degrees! Wilson was looking forward to the weekend. He was planning to go swimming and picnicking with his brother's family on Saturday. Then, on Sunday after church, he was going to watch the Indians' double-header on his friend's brand new big screen TV. He was thinking how glad he was that it hadn't been hot for last Tuesday night's game. It had been a perfect baseball night.

As he went about his rounds, Wilson saw Carol and they talked about Sunday afternoon's double-header and the Indians' chances. He kept up a good pace and was on the forty-fifth floor. He had to carry two big bags of mail into an attorney's office, and it was hot. Wilson was wiping his brow, glad the day was almost over, when he came out of the attorney's office. Then, as he walked toward his mail cart—[Oh, no! You guessed it!]—there sat the monkey, right on top of it!

Now, Wilson was tempted to try to grab the little monkey, but the zoo had told the security guards that they should not try to touch the monkey. They should just try to keep it on one floor and call the animal rescue workers, who are sometimes called "dog catchers." Thinking about this, Wilson called the animal rescue emergency number and he called the building's security guards.

While Wilson was on the telephone, the little monkey jumped off the mail cart and ran down one of the hallways. Wilson followed him but did not run. Unfortunately, two of the lights were burned out in that hall, so he could hardly see. He continued to follow the monkey, who pushed open a door at the end of the hall. The door opened, and the monkey disappeared. The security guards and animal rescue workers had not yet arrived. So Wilson followed the monkey and nudged open the door—which had no name or identification on it. There, at a big, round table sat a woman. It was hard to believe, but by the way she was dressed and from what was on the table, Wilson thought, "This is crazy in a downtown office building, but she looks like a fortune teller in a movie."

The monkey sat on a stand beside the woman. He perched there still as a statue and stared at Wilson.

"There, there, my sweet little one," the woman said, as she petted the little monkey. Wilson was so surprised and really so stunned, he just stared at her with wide eyes.

Then, the lady looked at him and asked, "You want somethin', Honeydew?"

Wilson, stood there. He stared at the little monkey and looked at the lady. Then, he said, "The monkey. The monkey. I've been seein' him all week long!"

The lady replied, "Well of course, he don't like waitin' for his mail till you get all the way up here to the top floor! 'Seems like maybe some days, you should start at the top floor and work your way down, Honeydew!"

Wilson said, "Yes, Ma'am. I'm sorry about that, Ma'am. Maybe I'll try that."

He started backing out of the room, and the lady with the monkey looked at him and smiled. Then, she said, "Now you enjoy watchin' the Indians' double-header on that big screen TV on Sunday, ya hear?!"

Wilson laughed that the lady had predicted what he was thinking about. Then, he realized that his Indians' pennant was hanging out of his mailbag. To be polite, Wilson said 'Good-bye,' turned, and went back out the door into the hallway. When he came out of the long dark hall, he found the security guards, who were searching for him. Wilson looked at them and said, "Let's find some place to sit down. I found the monkey. I'll tell you about the monkey, but I don't know if you're going to believe me."

Talking Points for "The Mailman's Mystery"

- Wilson is a mailman who works in Cleveland, Ohio.
- His entire mail route is in a forty-five-story office building.
- One day, while Wilson was thinking about the upcoming Cleveland Indians' baseball game, he found a little monkey sitting on top of his mail cart.
- Before Wilson could call the building's security guards, the monkey disappeared.
- That night, Wilson had fun with his brother at the baseball game, and the Indians won!
- The next day, while Wilson was delivering mail, he found the monkey sitting on his mail cart, again.
- Then, on Friday of the same week, when Wilson was almost done delivering the mail, the monkey appeared again!
- Wilson quickly called the animal rescue workers and the building's security guards.
- Then, he followed the monkey down a long, dark hallway into a room where a lady was dressed like a fortune-teller from a movie.
- When Wilson asked the lady about the monkey, she replied that he doesn't like to wait all day long to get his mail. That's why he comes to the mail cart to look for it. The lady suggested that Wilson should sometimes deliver mail starting at the top floor of the building, rather than always starting down on the first floor.
- As Wilson turned to leave, the lady wished him well on the weekend when he would watch the Indians' double-header. She predicted what he might do—noticing the Indians' pennant on his mail bag.
- Now, Wilson must explain to the security guards about the monkey!

Page 61

3
Straightforward Stories for Mid-Level and Lower Functioning Elders

In this chapter, we present stories that are suited for individuals who have moderate to severe neurocognitive impairment or dementia. Typically, moderate-to-low functioning can be identified by using the Mini-Mental State Exam (MMSE; Folstein, Fostein, & McHugh, 1975). We regard scores under 15 to be typical of moderate-to-low functioning. About folks with MMSE scores below 8, we've run into more than one expert who questioned our use of stories in activities for folks with severe impairment. However, we approach care of persons who are low functioning in much the same way as Joyce Simard (2009). A person with severe neurocognitive impairment/dementia is still a person, and s/he may still respond to the types of things that were enjoyable earlier in life: favorite songs, good conversation (even if s/he cannot reciprocate with equally complex sentences), and the mention of pleasing events. In a storytelling session, someone who is low functioning might "cue in" to only one or two items in a story, but this can still be a useful and productive thing.

As an example, consider the following. Lauren directed an hour-long activity one evening with the central theme of "California." The group included fourteen persons in long-term, residential care—all of whom have neurocognitive impairment (i.e., with a current diagnosis of dementia, possible Alzheimer's disease, or probable Alzheimer's disease via a physician). Levels of functioning in the group are mixed from mid-level to low. Among them is a lady whom Lauren has known for more than four years, and she is low functioning (with an MMSE around 7). Using a pseudonym to protect her, we'll call her "Liz."

During the group session, Lauren showed a map of the U.S., pointing out California. The group discussed numerous facts about California, such as the state tree (the redwood), and then Lauren read the story "Simply Ernest" (from this book) to them. After that, the group played a trivia game called, "Treasure Chest" (which Lauren has described in Chapter 4 of her 2009-book, *Roses Grow in a Butterfly Garden*, also available through Clove Press LTD). The Treasure Chest trivia items were all related to California, and some of them were, specifically, about Ernest's story. A number of participants were very active in the "game," and even Liz responded to one trivia question, remarking that Ernest had been looking at 'lights in the water.'

After the activity session, Lauren was pushing Liz in her wheelchair back toward her room and stopped just shy of the doorway to Liz's room. Turning away from Liz for a second in order to answer another resident's question, Lauren noticed that Liz had "pedaled herself" past the door to her room. When Lauren remarked to Liz that she had gone past her own room, Liz responded, "Of course! I'm going to California!"

Brilliant! Sometimes, we just expect that "nothing is getting in," but we are very often mistaken. See "Simply Ernest" in this Chapter. It is a very entertaining story and a favorite of activity participants in Lauren's weekly group for folks with neurocognitive impairment/dementia.

About Wording and Language

The stories in this section tend to be short with simple language. They are not intended to be literary masterpieces. Instead, they are designed to convey messages about enjoyable and interesting life events without complex sentence constructions. A number of them, such as "Waiting For Gammy" can be used quite easily in inter-generational programming. For example, a tea party might be arranged for ladies and their grandchildren (and/or great-grandchildren). Reading this story—with props, like a cute blue puppet or plush animal—might be especially entertaining!

Waiting For Gammy
by Lauren Smerglia Seifert

Denise is three years old, and her mommy works as a nurse for a pediatrician in the city. Monday through Friday, Denise's mother takes the train into the city to work and every morning Denise's "Gammy" comes over to take care of her while her mommy is out working.

"Gammy" is Denise's grandmother, and she always has fun things planned for them to do. Sometimes they fly kites in the park. On rainy days, they play "tea party" and dress up like fine ladies. Denise's baby dolls also attend the tea party in their finest clothes. They sit around a little table—with soda crackers on their tiny plates and chocolate milk in their cups, rather than tea.

On Tuesday morning, Denise stood in front of the big picture window in the living room. She looked out, asking, "Mommy, where is Gammy?"

"She will be here soon, Denise," Mommy replied.

After a few moments, Denise noticed Gammy's red hat in the distance. Here came Gammy up the sidewalk, and she was carrying a big box!

Denise jumped up and down and said, "Hurray! Hurray! Gammy is here!"

As Gammy came in the front door, she set the big box down in the front hallway and took off her coat. She pulled off her red gloves and hat. Then, she reached down to the big box, opened it, and took out a big blue, furry thing.

"What is it? What is it?" Denise asked, hopping around with excitement.

Gammy said, "It is a puppet. Do you know what a puppet is?"

"Yes," Denise responded. Then, she said, "No. No. What is it? What is a puppet?"

"Well, Sweetheart, a puppet is a type of doll that you can move in order to make it seem as if it can talk. This puppet has a space, so that I can put my hand up inside it and make its mouth move," Gammy explained. As she spoke, she showed Denise where to put her hand so that she could make the puppet's mouth move.

Denise pulled her arm back and said, "I don't understand, Gammy."

Gammy hugged Denise tightly to reassure her and said, "I will show you how it works. Let's go sit in the living room."

In the living room, Gammy picked up Denise and placed her on her lap. With Denise on Gammy's right knee, the puppet could rest on Gammy's left knee. Gammy put her arm up inside the blue furry puppet and moved its mouth. She made the puppet "talk."

In a silly, high-pitched voice, the puppet asked, "Denise, how are you, today?"

Denise looked at the puppet's moving mouth and laughed. Then, she answered, "I am fine, Mr. Puppet. How are you?"

STRAIGHTFORWARD STORIES

Page 65

"I am fine and dandy," replied Mr. Puppet.

Then, Denise asked, "What do you want to do today, Mr. Puppet?"

He responded, "I would like to build a fort in the living room. Do you want to help me?"

Denise hollered, "Yes! Yes! Yes!"

So, Gammy, Denise, and Mr. Puppet went upstairs to the linen closet and pulled out three big blankets. Then, with Mr. Puppet still hanging from her arm, Gammy started to arrange the blankets across the couch and love seat in the living room. She made it seem as if Mr. Puppet were holding a blanket in his mouth and helping by pulling the blanket across the furniture. Then, Denise, Gammy, and Mr. Puppet crawled on the floor, in order to enter the fort by going under the blankets.

When they were inside the fort, Denise said, "Gammy, I'm hungry."

"I will get a cracker for you, Honey!" Gammy said.

Gammy went out of the fort, leaving Mr. Puppet behind with her little granddaughter, Denise. Going to the kitchen, Gammy found a box of crackers and reached in to get one. She went back to the living room and got down on the floor—crawling back into the fort made of blankets. Then, she quietly laughed. Her adorable granddaughter had fallen asleep in the midst of the blankets—with her right arm inside Mr. Puppet. It seemed as if she had been trying to make him talk and then became so tired that she fell asleep.

Very carefully, Gammy picked up the tiny child and carried her—with Mr. Puppet—to bed. She tucked her in and laid Mr. Puppet down beside the sleeping child. Then, she kissed Denise's forehead and left her, so that she could nap.

That afternoon, Denise and Gammy dressed up Mr. Puppet in a pink feather boa with a black top hat. They dressed up, too, in pretty red hats and had a wonderful tea party. They ate crackers, and Gammy showed Denise how to make it seem as if Mr. Puppet were eating, too, by moving his mouth. Denise laughed and slapped her knee.

"Gammy, he is so funny! I know that he is just pretend, but when you move his mouth, it looks like Mr. Puppet is really eating!" giggled Denise.

Later that day, when Denise's mommy arrived home from work, the little one had a lot to say about the fun day with Mr. Puppet. As Gammy packed Mr. Puppet in the big box, Denise said, "Gammy, I can't wait for tomorrow. Maybe you will bring Mr. Puppet again!"

Gammy smiled and said, "Maybe! Maybe!"

The next morning—early—the little three-year-old stood at the window: watching and waiting for her gammy. As she waited, she said to her mommy, "I wonder what fun I will have with Gammy today!"

…And, of course, whatever they did, it was fun!

STRAIGHTFORWARD STORIES

Talking Points for "Waiting For Gammy"

- Denise is three years old, and her mommy is a nurse.
- Her "Gammy" babysits her each day when her mommy is at work.
- They have tea parties and play dress-up.
- One day, Gammy showed Denise a big, blue furry puppet.
- They made a fort, and Denise fell asleep in the fort.
- Denise and Gammy also had a tea party on that day, with Mr. Puppet dressed in a pink feather boa and a black top hat.
- Denise is excited to find out what Gammy will bring to play with tomorrow.

The following version of "The Kissing Wall" is different than the one presented in Chapter 2. This one is simpler and written to suit persons with moderate-to-severe neurocognitive impairment/dementia.

The Kissing Wall
by Virginia L. Smerglia

The town of River Bend is located at a beautiful point on the Ashland River. In fact, it is so beautiful that visitors to the town often say things like, "What a heavenly spot!" The surrounding hills are covered with forests and meadows. The trees change with the seasons and wildflowers and birds add every color. So, the views are heavenly!

As you might guess from the name, "River Bend," the town is in a place where the Ashland River curves. In fact, the river curves so much that the town is a peninsula. Part of the town faces east and part faces west. Some of the town's residents see the sun rise in the east and some see the sun set in the west. So, through the years, people have called these two areas of the town "Sunrise" and "Sunset." They're used to saying things like, "I live in Sunrise" or "I'm going to see friends over in Sunset."

The town's layout has stayed pretty much the same throughout its two-hundred-year history. This is because besides occupying a very beautiful spot, River Bend has been protected from floods. The Ashland River's current is not too swift, and the town sits a little above the river.

Part of the town is a park on the river bank in the Sunset area. This beautiful park, called Sunset Park, has been there about as long as the town. Here, the sunsets change according to the season. They tend to be pink and blue in spring and summer, golden and orange in fall, and blue and violet in winter. The sunsets in the park are so very beautiful that unless it is cloudy, there is usually an audience of town residents in cars and on park benches. It rests the mind and gives peace to the soul to sit there and watch the colors of the sky at sunset.

In the park, about two hundred feet back from the water's edge, is a stone wall which has been there as long as anyone can remember. The wall is made of smooth river stones of many colors: gray, brown, red, even a sort of blue. It is about three and a half feet high.

There are some town legends about the wall. One is that the wall was built by early settlers to discourage large animals like bears from coming into town. The settlers believed animals would hunt further downstream rather than trying to get over or around the wall. It's interesting that there are no tales about whether the wall was a success at keeping animals out of town, but it is a tradition to refer to the wall's ability, like saying that something is as likely to happen "as a bear coming over the wall at sunset." When a town's person says such a thing, she or he means that something isn't very likely to happen.

A second tradition is that the wall is where young lovers share their first kiss. Of course, that's where the wall got its name. It is called the "kissing wall." Also, there have been many marriage proposals there. So, the wall is quite a romantic place and many couples have carved their initials into the trees nearby.

Angela and Kevin Thayer are one of the town's well-known couples who got engaged at the kissing wall. Angela is the forty-four-year-old mayor of River Bend. And, people love to say her name: "Mayor Thayer." If there's a problem, like too many mosquitoes in summer or too many chuckholes in winter, someone is sure to remark, "Well, what did Mayor Thayer thay?" And, Mayor Angela Thayer takes the joke in good humor.

Here's the story of Angela and Kevin and the kissing wall. Twenty-one years ago, on a beautiful warm July evening, Kevin Thayer showed up at Angela's house with a box of fast-food fried chicken and a bottle of champagne and asked if she would like to join him for a picnic supper in the park. She was twenty-three at the time and just finishing her first year as a junior accountant at the local hospital. She and Kevin had been high school sweethearts. Their college years separated them. They had been far apart, and they dated other people. After college, they came home to find they were still soul mates.

So on this July night, Angela was a little shocked but very happy when Kevin, nervous and shaking, perched her on top of the kissing wall and brought out the champagne and a diamond ring. Angela was surprised, because Kevin had just finished his training at the police academy. That's right. He was a brand new policeman—on the job for only a few months. Angela thought he might want to get more experience in his new career before making any more big decisions. But, she later found out that Kevin was worried. He was afraid one of the young doctors at the hospital where she worked might ask Angela out and he thought a rookie cop couldn't compete with a doctor!

Now, twenty-one years later, Angela is the mayor of River Bend. She has been mayor for six years. Kevin is a detective in the police department, and they have two daughters, Mattie, age ten, and Della, age seven.

The thing that occupies Angela's mind these days is a very large dilemma for her and for the town council. They have decisions to make which could change their town. The decisions they have to make concern the kissing wall. How can this charming stone wall which is an important part of the town's history be involved in a huge problem?

TELMIA

The problem with the kissing wall is that it is no longer safe to sit on. It is very old—maybe over a hundred years—and a few rocks have fallen off the top. The bottom is unstable, too. One group of citizens wants the wall to be taken down so that there is no chance of someone getting hurt. However, other citizens say the wall is history and should be left as it is. They say the town can put up signs that announce the wall as unsafe to sit or lean on. They don't want the wall that was enjoyed by so many of their ancestors to be destroyed.

Before the town council meeting, the members have read the opinions on both sides of the issue. On the night of their meeting, Mayor Thayer says, "I know this is hard. We don't want to lose our kissing wall. We want to be able to go there and watch the sunset just as our parents and grandparents did, and we want the wall to be there for our children and grandchildren. The wall links us with the past and the future. On the other hand, we certainly don't want anyone to be injured because the wall is unsafe. I have talked with many people in the town and I want to give you an idea that might solve our problem. I think this solution may satisfy everyone. I have talked with a builder who restores historic buildings. He says it is his business to take things apart and put them together exactly as they were, but like new. He and his workers can take the wall down and lay it out like a map. They would mark each rock's place. Then, they would put the wall back together with new, strong mortar. It will be our good old kissing wall, but the rocks will no longer fall off the top, and the bottom will not be unstable any more. The rocks will have new connections. What do you think?"

All the town council members rise to their feet with applause for their mayor's work on finding a good solution to their problem. Mayor Angela Thayer has found a way to save the kissing wall and make it safe. Her husband, Kevin, stands in the back of the town hall and applauds as well. He is very proud!

Talking Points for "The Kissing Wall"

- The town of "River Bend" is named for its location on the Ashland River.
- Two areas of the town are "Sunrise" and "Sunset."
- In the area of "Sunset" there is a beautiful park with a wall that people sit on to watch the sun as it goes down each day. The colors of the setting sun are awe inspiring.
- The wall in the park is called the "kissing wall," because it is a romantic place.
- Angela and Kevin Thayer were engaged at the kissing wall, and Angela is now the town's mayor.
- A problem has arisen, because the town's wall is crumbling. So, the town council has called a meeting in order to discuss the problem.
- Mayor Angela Thayer proposes a solution. The town will bring in a builder, who will carefully take the wall apart and put it back together again with new mortar.
- Everyone is very glad that their mayor has found a way to save this historic landmark.

Ferns
by Virginia L. Smerglia

    Lucille Robinson is a plant lover! She has many beautiful houseplants. She takes very good care of them. She knows just how much water, sunlight, and plant food to give each kind of plant. All of Lucille's friends and neighbors know she spends hours on her houseplants every day. She has all kinds of houseplants, but her favorites are the ferns. She keeps them green and lovely. She knows how to grow new ferns which is very difficult and time-consuming. In summer, she hangs her ferns on her front porch and she often gives fern plants as gifts. She likes to see the big smiles on her friends' faces when they receive one of her new little ferns planted in a beautiful pot.

    Lucille lives in a big old Victorian house that her grandfather built. Her house is painted light blue with trim that is dark blue and very dark red. Painted three colors, her house is decorated in true Victorian style! When Lucille's big front porch is filled with bright green hanging ferns in summer, her house is very beautiful. She enjoys sitting on her porch swing and waving at neighbors and looking at her plants. She thinks her grandfather would be proud to see the house he built looking so good. She loves living in this fine old family home with all of her wonderful plants.

    Every year, in Lucille's town, there is a summer festival. The festival is everyone's favorite summer event. There are pony rides for the children and plenty of good home-cooked food. Lots of homemade ice cream is served. There are many interesting ice cream flavors, but most people really love the vanilla ice cream served with fresh strawberries and real whipped cream.

    The festival also includes a houseplant competition. Town's people bring their most beautiful plants to enter into the contest. The plants are judged and awards are given to one plant in each category. African violets are all judged together. Then, the ivy plants are all judged together. Finally, the ferns are all judged together. The winning plants are pinned with blue ribbons, and the winners of the blue ribbons get their pictures in the newspaper and on posters all around town.

    You can imagine that Lucille is one person who enters her plants into the contest every year during the summer festival. Since she is most proud of her ferns, she always hopes to win the blue ribbon for the most beautiful fern. This year, she is entering her best Boston fern. It is so big that she has asked her neighbor, Thomas, to transport the fern to the festival in his pick-up truck. Lucille and Thomas carefully place the fern on a box in the back of the truck. It has to be on top of something so the fern fronds don't get damaged. Then, Lucille puts padding all around the box. They carefully transport the fern to the festival.

    They unload the fern at the plant competition. They put the fern on a pedestal

STRAIGHTFORWARD STORIES

Page 73

TELMIA

they brought with them, and Lucille looks around at other plants. There are a lot of beauties! Her plants are like babies to her. She hopes her Boston fern will win the competition this year. This is the first year she has brought her most loved fern. She has always been afraid something would happen to it. Her mother gave it to her when she was only twenty years old. Now that she is fifty-five, Lucille thinks her Boston fern is more lovely than ever. It's big, too. At five feet across, it's huge!

Lucille has clipped a little stained glass bird on the Boston fern as a decoration. It's a glass bluebird. She stands back to admire the plant and there sits the little glass bird like a jewel, shining in the filtered sunlight. Lucille checks with the person in charge to make sure the plants will be watched and protected for the night. She is assured that the plants will be safe.

Lucille offers to treat Thomas to supper at the town diner to repay him for all his help. Thomas accepts and they are off for a delicious meal and a cup of great coffee at the diner. After supper, Lucille goes home to prepare for the plant judging that will happen tomorrow.

On the day of the festival, Lucille gets dressed to go. She is very excited about the plant competition. She chooses to wear a pair of navy blue pants—with a blue blouse which is exactly the color of the bluebird on her Boston fern. She wants to look good standing next to her plant.

At the festival, the judges are walking around the plants. There are three judges: a woman who has written a book on the care of houseplants, a college professor who teaches art, and a farmer who has special training in recognizing plant diseases and healthy plants. Lucille thinks that each judge has valuable knowledge for judging plants. The book author knows all about every kind of houseplant; the art professor knows about color and beauty; and the farmer knows how to tell whether plants are healthy.

When it comes time for the judges to announce their decisions and tell which plants have won the blue ribbons, Lucille is nervous. She has her hands folded tightly. She wants to be a good sport if she doesn't win, so she is thinking hard about how to smile sincerely if someone else gets the blue ribbon. She thinks about the movie stars who don't win the Oscars. She thinks about the looks on their faces. Some of them look like sour-pusses! She doesn't want to look that way. She wants to be gracious and have a pleasant smile.

Lucille thinks that whoever wins for the best fern will be a person like herself, someone who loves growing ferns. It will be someone who appreciates the beauty of a healthy fern and who knows all about the kind of filtered sunlight a fern needs. The winner will be someone who understands that a fern will turn yellow if you give it too much water. It will probably be someone who enjoys having a fern hanging on his or her front porch or entryway. In fact, Lucille thinks that she would probably like to get to know that person who wins.

Suddenly, Lucille realizes that someone is saying her name over a loudspeaker. "Lucille Robinson, Lucille Robinson, you are the winner of this year's fern competition. There are thirty ferns here at the festival and yours is judged the most beautiful, the healthiest, and certainly it is the largest!"

Lucille steps forward to where the judges are holding her blue ribbon. She is shocked. The judges put the blue ribbon on her Boston fern just below the little glass bluebird. The bright green fern is truly lovely with the bluebird and the big blue ribbon on it. Lucille, stands beside her plant. In her blue blouse, she makes quite a picture as the news reporter snaps her photo.

Lucille holds the microphone up and looks out at all her friends and neighbors. She says, "Thank you so much. This Boston fern was given to me by my mother over thirty years ago. I don't look the same as I did thirty years ago, but my fern looks much bigger and as good as ever. Isn't that amazing! I miss my mother, but when I look at this beautiful plant, I feel her love. Thank you for giving me the blue ribbon for my most special fern of all!"

Talking Points for "Ferns"

- Lucille Robinson loves to grow plants, and her favorite plants are ferns.
- She lives in a beautiful Victorian house that her grandfather built.
- Lucille's house is decorated in true Victorian style. Painted in three colors, it is light blue, dark blue, and dark red.
- Every summer, Lucille's town has a summer festival. It includes a contest for people who grow plants.
- Lucille has entered her best Boston fern in the competition.
- Thirty years ago, Lucille's mother gave her this Boston fern as a gift.
- Now, the fern is huge and beautiful!
- Lucille's neighbor, Thomas, helps her to deliver the fern to the competition.
- Lucille clips a pretty glass bluebird onto the fern, and she dresses in blue on the day of the competition.
- Before she knows it, the winners are being announced, and Lucille wins the blue ribbon for the prettiest fern!
- It is a wonderful day, and winning the blue ribbon leads Lucille to remember her mother fondly.

Simply Ernest
by Virginia L. Smerglia

This story is about a man named Ernest Jordan who lives in California near the ocean. He is a man with a difficult job. He fixes and replaces the very high lights on highways—the pole lights that are so tall, they light up the whole area. Street lights on the expressway are 60 or 70 feet high or even higher.

Fixing the lights along the highway is a tough job, but Ernest loves it. He likes being above almost everything else. He can see for miles around, and he likes to fix things.

Ernest is part of a team. His partners are Larry and John. Ernest does all of the high work, because he enjoys it. Larry and John say that is fine. They are content to stay on the ground and operate the crane that takes Ernest high into the sky. They also direct traffic and run some of the equipment that Ernest is using.

The crane has a work bucket on it; maybe you've seen one. Sometimes, they're called "cherry pickers." Ernest is strapped into the bucket with a safety harness. He has a phone with him and he talks with his two partners on the ground. It's too far and too noisy to be able to yell down to them. That's why they need the phone. Ernest's job requires a lot of training, because fixing highway lights is complicated. He's very good at what he does.

Larry and John are not sure why Ernest enjoys being up so high all the time, except for the view. It's always a difficult job, especially when the weather is bad or the traffic is heavy, but those things don't seem to bother Ernest.

Even Ernest's wife and children don't really know why he likes it so much. His wife, Carolyn, has asked him, but he just says, "It's hard to explain." Ernest cannot put it into words. He just knows that he likes to be high up in the cherry picker fixing pole lights along the expressway.

Ernest and Carolyn have three children: Rosemary, Basil, and Cilantro. Yes, those are their names. Maybe you noticed their children's names are all spices. Carolyn says that when their first child was born, Ernest suggested the name Rosemary and she thought it was a good name. When their second child was born, Ernest suggested the name Basil. Carolyn thought that was a good name too, but she mentioned to Ernest, "Maybe people will say Rosemary and Basil are both spice names."

He said, "Well, that's great because spices make life interesting. A very boring meal can become wonderful with some spices."

Then, when their third child, another son, was born, Ernest said, "I think the name Cilantro fits him perfectly."

Carolyn wasn't so sure. "I've never heard of anyone named Cilantro," she said.

STRAIGHTFORWARD STORIES

Ernest replied, "It's a very special name. It sort of floats through the air… Cilantro…and it is a wonderful spice. Maybe our son will bring some wonderful spiciness to the world."

After that speech, Carolyn was convinced. Now, Rosemary, Basil, and Cilantro are no longer little children. Rosemary has just finished college, Basil is in college, and Cilantro is a senior in high school. They all know about their father's love of heights, but, like his partners and his wife, it surprises them.

TELMIA

One afternoon, Ernest, John, and Larry are repairing some freeway lights that are particularly high…seventy feet up. Ernest likes this. He says, "The higher I go, the more I can see."

It's taking him a long time and it's getting to be dusk, so John and Larry use the phone to call up to Ernest. John says, "Hurry it up, Ernest. We want to get home and take our work boots off."

Ernest responds, "Okay, I'm working on it."

A half-hour later it is getting pretty dark. Larry calls up again, "Hey, Ernest, are you almost done? The evening traffic is pretty heavy."

Ernest says, "Larry, I'm enjoying the view; I'll be done in five minutes." Ernest looks out and he can see the beaches and the soft waves lapping up on the shore. Most of the sun bathers have left. A few people walk arm-in-arm along the shore.

As Ernest prepares to call Larry to bring him down, he looks at the edge of the

Page 78

water and sees an orange and gold glow along the edge of the ocean. It looks like there are lights under the water that are lighting up the waves. "Hey, guys!" he calls on the phone. "You aren't going to believe what I'm seeing….The water is lit up in colors of orange and gold. It's so beautiful!"

Larry says, "Hey, Ernest, I have my camera in the truck. Let me send it up to you in the tool basket so you can take some pictures." Ernest gets Larry's camera and starts taking pictures.

Ernest calls his wife, Carolyn, and tells her what he sees. "Oh, Carolyn, the shoreline is so beautiful! It looks as if there are golden lights twinkling under the waves!"

After talking to her husband on the phone, Carolyn decides to call the local television station. They're always asking for citizens to call when something unusual happens. The next thing Larry and John know, there's a television news van pulling up behind them. The reporter and photographer jump out to ask questions. The reporter asks if the photographer can please go up in the work bucket with Ernest to take pictures for the evening news. John calls their boss who okays the idea. It just so happens that the local television photographer had worked as a phone line technician for five years, so he knows all about cherry pickers and how to work in them. Larry and John bring down the work bucket and up goes the photographer with Ernest.

When the photographer sees the beautiful color, which is sparkling brightly now that it's totally dark outside, he is in awe. His cell phone rings. The news reporters says there is a college professor on the phone who says the lights are coming from a certain kind of plankton that floats into shore once every few years. The photographer and Ernest look out over the beautiful ocean with its glowing golden and orange lights.

"It's hard to be upset about anything while looking out at this beautiful light show!" Ernest says.

"Yeah, you can say that again," answers the photographer.

John and Larry get into the truck and turn on the evening news. They have a small TV in their van, which they watch during their work breaks.

"Now for local news," says the commentator.

"Oh, I wanted to see the baseball scores," says John. However, his eyes pop at what they see and hear next.

The news commentator says, "We're talking by cell phone to Mr. Ernest Jordan who is seventy feet in the air repairing a light on the coast freeway. He is looking out at the ocean and he sees the water at the shoreline is glittering with orange and gold lights."

"What can you tell us, Mr. Jordan?" the commentator asks.

"It is beyond belief! From up here, it looks like a wonderful painting, a work of

God for sure," Ernest replies.

"Well, thank you, Mr. Jordan, and you be safe up there! You heard it here first, folks. The phosphorescent plankton are back, and they are making an amazing light show along the shoreline tonight!" adds the TV commentator.

John and Larry jump out of the truck and look up at Ernest. He gives them the signal to bring his work bucket down. When he and the photographer get to the ground, he looks at them. Ernest's eyes are glistening.

"We heard you on the news, " John says.

Ernest replies, "It's like being at a carnival and a Christmas light show all at once. It's shimmering and it makes the water look like it's not really water at all, but a glittering painting."

Ernest's cell phone rings just then and he hears Cilantro's voice, "Hey Dad, we saw you on TV talking about the glowing plankton in the water. It must be amazing to see such a thing from high up in the cherry picker. Oh, by the way, Mom says that dinner's ready, and we're having your favorite to celebrate your interview on the news tonight!"

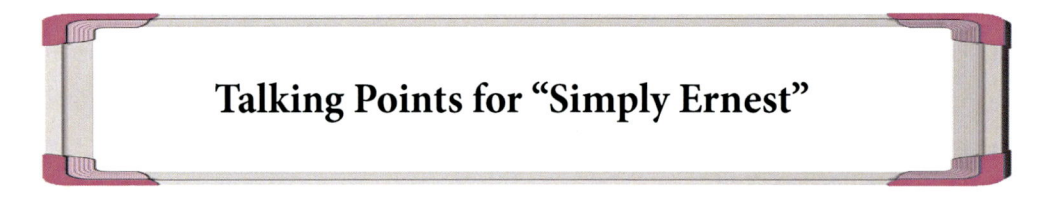

Talking Points for "Simply Ernest"

- Ernest, Larry, and John work together.
- They repair light poles along the highway in western California.
- A lot of their work happens along the coast highway, where they can see the ocean.
- Ernest likes to go high up in the "cherry picker" in order to repair the lights.
- Ernest's wife, Carolyn, and his three children (who are all named after spices!) do not understand why Ernest likes to work on light poles sixty to seventy feet off the ground.
- One afternoon, while Ernest is very high up, repairing a light, he sees an amazing thing in the ocean: glowing orange and golden lights.
- Ernest calls his wife, Carolyn, on the cell phone in order to tell her about the beautiful light show that is happening in the ocean.
- Ernest's wife calls the local TV station, and they send someone out to see the glowing waves.
- Ernest and the amazing ocean lights (from phosphorescent plankton) both end up on the evening news!

The Basket Factory
by Virginia L. Smerglia

If you have ever been to northern Virginia or southern West Virginia, you know there is a large area with beautiful mountains. They are part of the Appalachian Mountains; they are the part usually called the Blue Ridge Mountains, because they look blue from a distance. They are beautiful to see, and many people enjoy hiking or even driving hundreds of miles through the Blue Ridge Mountains. In the fall, of course, the mountains add many other colors as the leaves on the trees change to red, orange, and golden yellow.

All through the mountains are small towns. Most of them are in the valleys. In many of these towns, people know arts and crafts, which have been passed down through generations. Some people make beautiful quilts. Some people know how to make pottery that lasts for years and years. The pottery they make uses salt that originally came from salt mines in the area. The potters make useful things like pitchers and bowls. The colors are rich and beautiful, like blue that reminds people of the Blue Ridge.

TELMIA

Another skill that was handed down through the generations is basket making. Ash trees growing in the low areas are good for making basket strips for weaving. Each summer, the new wood is cut into strips, pounded flat, and used to weave baskets that last a long time. This story is about a basket factory in a town in northern Virginia. This town and the basket factory are made up, but there are many towns in the Blue Ridge Mountains just like this one.

In the town of Graystone, there is a basket factory. It is the Graystone Basket Factory. Many of the town's people work in the basket factory. The baskets are sold to tourists in gift shops in Virginia and West Virginia. They are expensive because it takes a lot of time and skill to make the strong baskets that last a lifetime. The baskets keep their beauty because they retain their shapes and colors, which come from dyes made of berries and plants.

It is sometimes difficult to convince tourists and other customers that things made in the old ways like quilts, pottery, and baskets are worth buying. These items seem expensive when compared with more cheaply made items, but the cheaper items don't last nearly as long.

Most of the workers in the Graystone Basket Factory can't do anything to help sell the baskets. They are busy making baskets all day. Even if they had more time, they wouldn't know what to do. So, the basket company has hired a man named Robert to help them sell baskets. Robert knows a lot about the value of the baskets, because he was born and raised in Graystone. Back then, everyone called him, "Bobby." Then, he went away to college and studied marketing. Now, he knows how to help companies sell their products, because he is a marketing consultant. Also, Robert has lost the nickname, "Bobby," because he is grown up and it no longer fits him. These days, the only people who still call Robert by his boyhood name are his mom and dad!

Today, Robert is going to speak to the executives of the Graystone Basket Factory. He has been invited to make a presentation that will give them some ideas of how to market their baskets. If they don't improve sales, some people will have to be laid off and that would be very bad for the town. Making baskets requires a lot of skill, but it is also very specialized work. It would be hard to find another job that would use their basket-making skills.

As he arrives for his meeting with the Directors of Graystone Basket Factory, Robert is nervous. He has a lot of marketing experience, but some of the older executives have known him since he was a child. So, Robert is concerned about whether they will respect his opinion or just think of him as "little Bobby" who used to mow their lawns.

When Robert goes into the conference room and sees the managers, he feels better. They seem to be pleased he is there. They greet him warmly. They are anxiously awaiting his help.

    Robert begins his presentation by saying, "The first thing I want to tell you is that the baskets are good, strong, and attractive—just as they have always been. You have done a good job at keeping up with the needs people have today. I especially like the bedside baskets you've developed for cell phones and video games. The new colors you have are what people want now. So I don't believe you need to change anything about the products you are making."

    The executives were very pleased to hear this!

    Robert went on to say, "The second thing I want to tell you is that I have studied the number of customers who come into the tourist and gift shops where you sell the baskets. I believe there are not enough people seeing your baskets in these stores. I have several suggestions to make. Then, you can discuss them and let me know what questions you have and whether you want to use any of my ideas."

    Robert continued, "There are many things you can do and most of them will require you to decide to spend some money. First, we can make a website so you can sell your baskets on the Internet. Nowadays, lots of people love to use their home computers to shop. Customers can go to the website, see the baskets, purchase them, and we can ship them. Second, I can approach some companies that sell things through catalogs. We can ask them to include some of your baskets. The best catalogs would be the ones that sell things for the home. Third, I can approach some chain stores that have stores all over the country to see whether they would carry your baskets. Fourth, we could just advertise more, put ads in magazines, on local television, and on billboards on the interstate. The big things to consider here are the costs of each of my ideas and also, when we are successful, will Graystone Basket Factory be able to keep up with suddenly having to make a lot more baskets?"

As Robert finished speaking, he answered a few questions, and gave out some information sheets. Then, he left and went back to his mom and dad's house. It was nice to have an excuse to come back to Graystone for a visit, and Robert was glad to think that he might be able to use his marketing skills to help his hometown. He was surprised when his cell phone rang only an hour after he left the meeting. He answered quickly and it was one of the executives from the Graystone Basket Factory asking him if he could come back right away.

When Robert got back to the basket factory and went into the conference room, everyone was very excited. They had opened the windows, because there was so much heat in the room. The president of Graystone Basket Factory, a woman named Lynne James, stood up immediately.

Lynne said, "Robert, thank you for your willingness to help us. We would like it if you would, first, go to one of the chain stores that sells nice home products for kitchen, bath, and bedroom. We think they will like our picnic basket, our sleigh basket for Christmas, our Easter baskets, and our bedside baskets. Of course, you can decide whether other products would interest them. We think it would be cost-effective, because they would carry the cost of advertising and shipping. If you can't interest a chain store, then we'll go back to the drawing board with ideas for a website. We have a website already, but it isn't interesting and we don't have anyone who knows how to keep it up."

Robert was so pleased that his ideas and expertise were acceptable to the executives of Graystone Basket Factory. He was glad that they would trust him to carry his plans forward. He felt sure he could help keep his hometown company from going downhill or even closing.

Robert was happy and a bit surprised that they placed so much trust in him, because he knew there was at least one executive there whose house he had egged during Trick-or-Treat when he was a child. The man had a son Robert's age and the two had been in a rivalry during their childhood years. In a prank, "little Bobby" had arrived one night and had thrown eggs at their windows.

As the meeting ended and Robert prepared to move forward with plans to help the Graystone Basket Factory, he walked over to that gentleman. A very grown-up Robert said, "Mr. Barlow, thank you so much for not holding an old Halloween prank against me!"

Mr. Barlow, the chief accountant for Graystone Basket Factory, responded, "Robert, you seem to know what you're doing. Your marketing degree and your reputation for helping companies seem to be excellent. Sure, I remember that you and my son used to get into all kinds of scrapes as kids, but after all, what are a few broken eggs between friends?"

With that, Mr. Barlow shook Robert's hand and Robert responded, "Thank you, Mr. Barlow."

To that, Mr. Barlow replied, "Call me Edward, please," and patting Robert on the back, he continued, "Now, get to work, Son, so that you can help us save the Graystone Basket Factory!"

Talking Points for "The Basket Factory"

- In Virginia and West Virginia there is an area known as the Blue Ridge Mountains.
- The Blue Ridge Mountains are part of the Appalachian Mountains.
- In the Blue Ridge, people have many skills, like making pottery, quilts, and baskets.
- These crafts and skills have been passed down through the generations.
- In the town of Graystone, many town's folk make baskets at the Graystone Basket Factory.
- The Graystone Basket Factory is struggling to stay in business, because their sales have dropped.
- Robert is originally from Graystone, and he has returned after going to college for a marketing degree. He is going to help the factory and the town.
- After presenting his ideas to the directors of the basket company, Robert discovers that they trust him to help them.
- Robert had gotten into some scrapes as a kid, like the time he egged Mr. Barlow's house.
- Back then, he was known as "little Bobby," but now, he is grown up and people call him Robert.
- In the end, President Lynn James, Mr. Barlow, and the other executives trust Robert to help them save the Graystone Basket Factory.

The Frogs
by Lauren Smerglia Seifert

Gordon and Jennifer have no children of their own, but they don't mind, because they spend many hours with their nieces and nephews. Although they work and live in the city, they are able to vacation for three—yes! three!—wonderful weeks in the summertime, and two of their nieces come to visit.

This year, Uncle Gordy and Aunt Jen (which is what the children call them) will once again play and have fun with Tina and Maria. They are the daughters of Jen's sister, and it will be a nice little break for their mom when the two girls visit their Uncle Gordy and Aunt Jen.

Gordy and Jen arrive at the rented cabin at Miller's Pond with groceries, bedding, and cleaning supplies. They spend a day just scrubbing up the place, so that it is ready for their two girls! They are so excited about spending time with their nieces! Gordon is especially happy that he will have his two "fishing buddies" again this year. He loves fishing with his two nieces!

On Saturday, Aunt Jen drives back into the city to pick up a few things they had forgotten, and then she goes to her sister's house in order to pick up her nieces. As Jen drives up, she can see that the girls are already out front waiting for her. Tina is 6, and Maria is 10 years old. Each one has a cute little suitcase and a sleeping bag.

Once they get on the road, the two little girls are like chatterboxes in the backseat. They want Aunt Jen to tell them all the things that they will do on their vacation, but Aunt Jen says, "Well, you'll just have to wait and see. Vacation is a time of surprises!"

Back at the cabin, Uncle Gordy gets big hugs from his two nieces and he helps them unpack their suitcases. Aunt Jen makes a lunch of peanut butter and jelly sandwiches with celery and apple slices. Afterward, they all head down to the big Miller's Pond to clean up the boat and find out whether she is "sea worthy." Once the boat is clean, they decide that fishing will be at the top of their list of things to do!

Tina and Maria love to fish with their Uncle Gordy. First, the girls must put on their life jackets. Then, Uncle Gordy checks to be sure that there is enough gas in the engine, then he takes them out on the boat and sets them up with their fishing rods. Once the girls have their lines in the water, Gordy leans back and dozes off. After a while, one of the girls gives a holler that she thinks a fish is tugging on her line, and Uncle Gordy leaps to his feet in order to help her bring the fish in. Usually they use worms as bait, but this year, Gordy has been growing little frogs, and he anticipates that they will bring in some nice big fish for frying. Even though they are at "Miller's Pond" the name is funny, because the pond is actually a nice, big lake! The fish are pretty big, too, and the right bait can bring in fish that are large enough for supper!

Uncle Gordy explains to the girls that he has some good bait for them. "It's frogs!" he exclaims.

"Frogs????" asks Maria with a look of surprise.

"Well, you know how we used worms as bait last year, Maria?" asks Uncle Gordy as both girls nod. "Well, we didn't catch any nice big fish for supper. This year, I want to try some little frogs, in order to see whether we can catch some large frying fish," he says as he holds out his arms to indicate the length of a big fish.

"Oh, good," Tina says, clapping. "We can have fish for supper!"

While Uncle Gordy, Tina, and Maria go out on the boat and fish, Aunt Jen stays back at the cabin, so that she can make up the beds and tidy up. Once Uncle Gordy has shown the girls the container of frogs, he sets up their lines and puts the container of croaking frogs between them. Then, he sits back in his chair and resumes his little nap. He is very surprised that the fish aren't biting. Not once, does either of the girls holler for help with her line. After three hours, they go swimming and then head back across the water. They are sad to report to Aunt Jen that there are no fish for dinner.

"That's OK," Aunt Jen consoles them. "I have hot dogs, and you can try again for frying fish tomorrow."

Three days in a row, Uncle Gordy takes the girls out fishing, and three days in a row, they use up the whole container of frogs without catching so much as a blue gill! On the fourth day, Aunt Jen decides to go with them on the boat.

"Maybe, I can be your good luck!" she says happily. "I'll help you to catch a nice big fish for supper."

When the four get out into the open water, Uncle Gordy sits back in his chair and takes a cat-nap, while Aunt Jen baits her hook with one of the frogs. As she does this, and casts off, her two nieces look on in disbelief. Tina and Maria's eyes are wide as they stare at their aunt.

"Oh, no," mutters Tina.

"What's wrong, Honey?" asks Aunt Jen as she looks at her little niece with concern.

"That poor little frog," replies her other niece, Maria.

"What do you mean, Sweetheart?" questions Jen. "Isn't this how you have been baiting your hooks during these past three days? This is how we catch the big fish!"

Both nieces shake their heads and look down at their feet and the bottom of the boat. Then, Tina says, "No, Aunt Jen. We just couldn't bear to see those cute little frogs get eaten by big fish. Each day, when we were sure that Uncle Gordy wasn't watching anymore, we set all those cute little froggies free—right back into the water—where they can swim and be happy again!"

Well, this certainly explains why they hadn't been catching any fish for the past three days! Jen doesn't tell the two sweet girls that frogs in the water—swimming freely, instead of on a fishing hook—are still a nice meal for a big fish. Instead, she smiles and kisses each of her nieces on the forehead.

Aunt Jen giggles and says, "Well, fishing hooks without any bait on them. Huh. That is why you haven't been catching fish. Leave it to me, girls. I'll catch us a nice big one!"

With that, Jen feels a tug on her line. She reels it in to find a trout! It is a good size and will be excellent when cooked on the fire back at the cabin. Jen pulls her line in, wrestles the fish into the cooler, and baits the hook with another frog. Within about five minutes, she has reeled in another good-sized fish, and after that, she brings in two more. Now, there were three frogs left in the bait container.

"Aunt Jen?" Maria questions. "Do you have to use all of them? Can't we let these three little froggies go so that they can be happy?"

Jen looks at her two nieces. Their wide eyes and adorable little faces are just too much for her. She decides to allow them to "free" the last three frogs from the bait container. After all, they now have enough fish for dinner. Jen hands the bait container to her nieces and watches as they dump the leaping frogs from the plastic bin into the water.

Tina yelps, "Hurray! The frogs are free!"

With that, Uncle Gordy awakens from his nap just in time to see the frogs jumping from the container into the water. He is surprised and very interested as Aunt Jen explains to him why they hadn't caught any fish during the past three days.

For many years after that—even after the girls had grown up—they would laugh and tell the story about the mystery of three days of fishing when no fish were caught.

Uncle Gordon would laugh and say, "And all the time, they were fishing without any bait, because they had set all the little frogs free!"

And everybody would laugh, because those vacation days were some of the most fun days ever.

Talking Points for "The Frogs"

- Gordon and Jennifer work in the city.
- During August of each year, they vacation in a cabin at Miller's Pond.
- Gordon and Jennifer have no children of their own, but they love to spend time with their nieces and nephews, who call them "Uncle Gordy" and "Aunt Jen."
- Jennifer's sister has two daughters: Tina, who is 6, and Maria, who is 10.
- Tina and Maria love to spend part of August with their Uncle Gordy and Aunt Jen.

- Tina and Maria are Uncle Gordy's "fishing buddies."
- Last year, Tina, Maria, and Uncle Gordy used worms as bait and caught only little fish.
- This year, Uncle Gordy has little frogs that they will use as bait. He wants to catch some big fish and fry them for supper.
- They fish for three days but catch nothing!
- On the fourth day, Aunt Jen goes fishing with them and discovers that the girls have been letting the frogs loose, rather than using them as bait!
- No wonder they haven't caught any fish. They were fishing without bait!
- Aunt Jen shows the girls how to fish with frogs as bait, and she lets them free a few of the frogs, too.
- Many years after that, Uncle Gordy, Aunt Jen, Tina, and Maria still have fun telling the story about how the girls let the frogs loose and fished without any bait.

A Giraffe In The Barn
by Virginia L. Smerglia

This story is about a farm family. They live on a farm in Western Pennsylvania, and their last name is unusual. It is "Storm!" The father is Sonny Storm; he is forty-seven years old. His wife is Sandy Storm, and their kids are sixteen-year-old twins named Misty and Hale Storm. That's right. Sonny and Sandy named one of their twins: "Hale Storm!"

Now, the farm has been in the Storm family for five generations. It is beautiful, with rolling hills, streams, and thick woods. Sonny recalls his happy childhood: hiking in the woods, fishing in the streams, and helping his parents with planting and harvesting. One exciting thing in Sonny's childhood was a big Halloween party with all the neighbors. They held the Halloween party every year after the harvest. It would usually be in someone's barn and they would bob for apples and make caramel corn.

Sonny's favorite thing about growing up on a farm was the animals. He enjoyed waking up every morning to feed them. He would talk, and the cows would "moo" back at him. The sheep would answer, too, with "baa" when they saw him. When baby calves, lambs, and pigs were born, Sonny was allowed to name them. His parents enjoyed the fact that Sonny did have a way with animals.

The Storms' farmhouse is where Sonny now lives with Sandy and their twins. This old farmhouse was built by Sonny's great-great-grandfather, and Sonny likes to make a joke about it. He tells people, "This house has been through many, many Storms and it's still standing!"

The Storm's Victorian farmhouse has a porch that goes all the way around it. On the porch set wicker rocking chairs and big flowerpots—just like you see in the movies. There is a sort of square tower on top of the house. You can actually go up in the tower from the attic and look all around the countryside. Sonny's parents told him that in the early days the tower was used as a lookout. The Storm Family would use the tower to watch for the stagecoaches that would come through on their way to Ohio and the West.

After high school, Sonny went to college. He was bored by the courses he took in accounting and business. He looked forward to coming home on his breaks from college, so he could be outside in the fields and woods. He would spend time in the barns with the animals. When he went back to school again, he really missed the farm.

Sonny's dad said to him, "I know you might not like some of those college courses, but when you get your business degree in farm management, you can come home and run the farm with all the new techniques I don't know about."

Well, that is exactly what Sonny did. He learned how to run a modern farm and came home and did a great job of it. Even though it is very difficult, he has been doing it successfully for over twenty years.

    Sonny still loves the animals most of all, and he is always looking for something new. For example, he brought some llamas to the farm a few years ago and later he got some peacocks, which strut around and keep the place lively with their bright colors and their loud squawks. Those loud peacocks are always surprising to visitors at the farm. For some reason, most people think that peacocks don't make noise, but they sure do!

    Lately, Sonny has been thinking about something unusual he wants to do. He's reluctant to tell his family and friends, because he expects they may think his idea is silly. He wants to have a giraffe on his farm, because he loves giraffes. Even as an adult, he always enjoys seeing them at the zoo. Sonny says that giraffes have kind eyes and they look as though they need love. He has read that they can see a human being a mile away, and they see colors. He has also read that they are the most peaceful animals on earth, and he really likes that idea. He has looked into whether a giraffe can live in a climate with cold winters. After all, if Sonny were to bring a giraffe to his farm, it would have to be able to survive the cold Pennsylvania winter in their barn! While doing some research on giraffes, Sonny found out that they do just fine in zoos all over the world. In fact, giraffes even seem to like the winter—as long as they are inside when it is colder than forty degrees.

Sonny talks his idea over with his wife Sandy. Together, they decide to put an ad on the internet to find out if anyone has a giraffe to sell. He is amazed to receive several replies. One that sounds promising is from a family in Ohio. Evidently, the Coopers in Ohio have quite a few unusual animals. They are selling them now, because they are moving to Australia. As it turns out, the Coopers live only three hours from the Storm family farm. So, Sonny calls and asks whether he can come and visit the giraffe. The Coopers agree, and they invite the whole Storm family to come visit on the following Saturday.

That's how Sonny and Sandy and the twins meet Esther Moon, a four-year-old, fourteen-foot tall giraffe from Ohio. It is love at first sight! Esther Moon bends down to take apples from Misty's and Hale's hands.

"Woe!" says Hale. "That's a pretty long purple tongue!"

"It's almost two feet long," says Mrs. Cooper. "It has to be so she can eat leaves and bark from high up in the trees."

Misty asks, "Does that mean we'd have to leave her in the woods, so that she can eat trees?"

"Oh, no," laughs Mr. Cooper. "You would want to give her grain feed, fruit, and vegetables. It is when giraffes live in the wild that they eat the high young leaves from acacia trees."

Esther Moon bends down and blinks her long eyelashes at the Storm twins. She wants more fruit. They give her some more apples, pat her face, and rub her neck. That does it! Within an hour, Sonny and Sandy are making arrangements to buy Esther Moon and transport her to their farm. They plan to build a special building just for her. Sonny wants to build the barn and paint it green before Esther arrives in Pennsylvania. The Coopers say they will leave for Australia in six months. So they are happy to keep their favorite animal until Sonny has the building ready.

When Esther Moon's new tall, green home is ready, Sonny contacts several big zoos and finds one that is happy to help them move Esther Moon to the Storm Farm in Pennsylvania. Once she has time to settle in, friends, neighbors, and even a lot of people the Storm family doesn't know want a chance to see Esther Moon. Sonny has anticipated this, building her house not too far from the road. It's close enough so that people can see her, but not so near to the road that she will be bothered by all the traffic and people.

Esther Moon's house has a large play area where she can come out and eat and run around a bit. Since giraffes can run as fast as thirty-five miles an hour, Sonny plans to let her out into the meadow once she gets accustomed to her new house. She will need to get exercise, so that she stays healthy.

TELMIA

The Storms are now used to having cars in front of their house and people knocking at the door to ask if they can take a picture of "Esther Moon: The Giraffe." Just as Sonny has always believed, giraffes do have kind eyes and they do need love. Esther Moon likes to bat her eyelashes and show off for visitors. Some people even believe she is smiling at them. Oh, and, guess what? Esther Moon's house has a tower on it just like the Storms' house, so that she can see the countryside!

The local newspaper sends a reporter to interview Sonny and take pictures of Esther Moon. When the paper comes out, the headline reads, "A GIRAFFE WHO ENJOYS STORMS!!"

Talking Points for "A Giraffe In The Barn"

- Sonny and Sandy live on their family farm in Pennsylvania.
- They have twins: Misty and Hale.
- Their last name is "Storm."
- On the Storms' family farm, there are many animals, and there is a beautiful Victorian farmhouse.
- Sonny Storm's family has lived on the farm for five generations, and Sonny loves animals.
- Sonny went to college to learn business techniques for running the farm.
- Now, Sonny runs the farm, as he has done for more than twenty years.
- Because he loves giraffes, Sonny decides to buy one.
- He takes the family to Ohio to visit the Coopers, who have a giraffe they want to sell.
- Esther Moon is a beautiful, fourteen-foot tall giraffe.
- The Storms fall in love with her, and she seems to like them, too.
- Sonny Storm makes arrangements for Esther Moon to be transported to the Storm Family Farm, and he builds a tall, green house for her.
- From then on, people come from miles around in order to meet "Esther Moon: The Giraffe."
- Because of the family's name, the local newspaper calls Esther, "A GIRAFFE WHO ENJOYS STORMS!!"
- For more information about giraffes, visit the sites where we found some of the details at: www.nationalzoo.si.edu/Animals/AfricanSavanna/fact-giraffe.cfm and www.cmzoo.org/exhibitsAttractions/giraffes/giraffeFacts.asp

Fishing For Romance
by Lauren Smerglia Seifert

Of all the ways that two people can meet, James and Miranda met on a boat ramp. It was 7:00 P.M. on a Tuesday, and James was pulling his fishing boat up out of the water at Lake Milton. He had taken a half-day vacation from work in order to go fishing with his brother, Tom. They had headed out after lunch to find out if any fish were biting. They fished from 2:00 P.M. until 7:00 P.M.

As they were pulling the fishing boat out of the water and securing it to the trailer on the back of their truck, James looked up to see the most beautiful woman he had ever cast his eyes upon. It was Miranda. She and her sister had decided to take an evening walk at the lake. As they hiked along, they decided to take a different path than usual—strolling over to the boat launch in order to look out at the boats.

As James and Tom hauled their fishing boat up onto the trailer, Miranda looked out across the murky green water. She smiled and asked, "Did you catch anything?"

James looked at her with his blue eyes sparkling. He held up a string of fish, grinned, and replied, "The fish were biting. We caught dinner!"

Thinking it would be the end of this brief exchange with strangers, Miranda said, "Well, that is super! Those fish ought to be a delicious supper."

James didn't want to let the opportunity pass, because he thought Miranda was the most lovely lady he had ever seen, so he stammered, "They will be delicious. We were just going to clean them and cook them up on the grill. Would you like to join us for a picnic?"

As Miranda's auburn brown hair shined with the sun behind it, she answered with a wink and said, "Well, that would be just fine. Thank you."

James and Tom pulled their truck and trailer up off the boat launch and into a parking space. Then, they gathered their ice chest and walked with Miranda and her sister, Dorothy, up to the park benches and picnic area. Miranda offered to set the table as James cleaned the fish and Tom grilled them. As they prepared supper by the lake, the two sisters discovered that they had much in common with the two brothers. Miranda and Dorothy had grown up nearby, and so had James and Tom. They had all spent a lot of time on Lake Milton as children: boating, swimming, and fishing. However, somehow they had never met.

Miranda told them, "Our mom and dad live just around the bend on the east shore."

James responded, "Well, our mom lives on the west shore!"

Miranda's sister laughed and said, "No wonder we've never met. You're from the other side of the lake!"

They all laughed. They enjoyed the scrumptious grilled fish with some potato salad that Tom had brought along in the ice chest, and it seemed as if this was a supper made in heaven. It certainly was! James and Miranda had hit it off, and Tom and Dorothy soon started dating, too. A year later, both couples were married, and friends marveled that a chance meeting along the lakeside could have led two brothers to marry two sisters. They always joked about the day that Miranda and Dorothy decided to take a different path on their evening walk and ended up finding two fishermen for husbands!

Talking Points for "Fishing For Romance"

- James and Tom are brothers who went fishing.
- Miranda and Dorothy are sisters who took an evening walk.
- The brothers met the sisters at Lake Milton's boat ramp.
- James and Tom had caught some fish for supper.
- They invited Miranda and Dorothy to join them for grilled fish.
- This chance meeting led Miranda and James to start dating.
- Tom and Dorothy started dating soon afterward.
- A year later, the two brothers were married to the two sisters!

Meeting a TV Star
by Virginia L. Smerglia

This story is about a kindergarten teacher named Bridget Cane. After school one day, she was walking to her car with a friend named Kate.

Bridget looked at her friend and said, "Taking care of kindergarteners all day is exhausting! I'm so tired that I don't have the energy to eat supper. I'm even too tired to sleep!"

Kate laughed and said, "So, you're too tired to sleep? That's a new one!"

Kate is a teacher too, but her students are fifth-graders. She doesn't have the physical work that Bridget does. Bridget has to tie shoelaces, zip jackets, and help the kindergartners to the bathroom.

As they walked to their cars after school, Kate said, "I'll tell you what, Bridget. I will treat you to a pizza. You go ahead home, take a shower, and get into your jammies. I'll meet you there in a half hour. We can eat our pizza, watch some TV, and then I'll go home, so that you can crawl under the covers."

"Sounds like heaven to me," said Bridget. "I like pepperoni and not too much sauce. Thank you, Kate."

Kate smiled and replied, "Like I might forget, Bridget. We've only shared a couple thousand pizzas together in the last four years!"

Bridget said, "Wow! It is four years that we've been teaching at Bentley School. Can you believe it? Four years, Kate! It seems like two at most. I guess it's because the weeks and months fly past like those clouds up there."

Bridget pointed at the clouds overhead. As the two young teachers walked toward their cars, they saw dark storm clouds gathering.

"It'll be a great night to stay in and be cozy. I'll see you at your apartment!" Kate called.

Bridget got home and laid everything out that she wanted to wear the next day: blue slacks, a blue top, and a vest. Her kindergartners were studying blue and she was planning an all-blue wardrobe to help them learn. She also got out some blue lollipops and put them in her bag for the next day's class. Finally, she tossed her dirty clothes in the hamper, took a shower, and put on her pajamas. By then, the storm outside was really beginning to howl! She thought of Kate out in the storm and hoped she'd arrive soon.

Bridget was just beginning to worry about Kate when the doorbell rang. In her pajamas and bathrobe, she ran to the door and yelled, "Hey, Kate, I thought you'd never get here."

But as Bridget opened the door, she was surprised to see one of her kindergarten students. Five-year-old Taylor was standing at her door, with a very handsome man next to her. They were drenched with rain! As Bridget stared at them, she realized that the man was not only handsome, he was a TV star! She recognized him as an actor who plays a brave fireman on a television show she had seen. Now, Bridget was very embarrassed to be in her pajamas at 5:00 P.M. She thought of all the great outfits she might have worn if she had known a very, very handsome TV star was going to knock on her door.

"Taylor, hello! I'm surprised to see you!" Bridget said as she beckoned to the rain-soaked pair to come inside.

TELMIA

The little girl looked sheepish. The actor said, "Sorry to barge in like this, Miss Cane. I'm Sam. I'm Taylor's daddy. We live just a few blocks from here and we were walking home when the storm caught us without an umbrella. Taylor saw your light on, and she suggested that we might ask you for shelter from the storm. Perhaps, we could even borrow an umbrella?"

Bridget smiled. She liked Taylor—a very shy little girl. Sam was a single dad, raising Taylor alone. She knew Sam traveled a lot and that his sister was helping to raise the little girl. Now that she had seen him, she realized why he was out of town so much. His job as a TV star probably kept him very busy!

"Please, come in out of the wind. That rain is coming down in torrents!" Bridget said.

Sam brought Taylor in and Bridget took their raincoats and hung them to dry in the laundry room.

"Well," she said, "I don't usually dress in my pajamas at supper time, but today was such a long day. I just thought I'd go right to bed. I apologize for being so informally dressed! I'm happy to meet you, Sam, and to tell you that Taylor is doing so well in kindergarten. She can already read several books, and she has only been in school two months!"

Sam looked very pleased and Taylor grinned at her dad.

Just then, there was a knock on the door and in walked Kate with a huge pizza box. "Hey, Bridget, I brought salads, too. Oh, dear! I didn't realize you have company." Kate gasped and her eyes looked like they might pop across the room and stick on Sam.

After introductions, Bridget saw the jumbo pizza and said, "Sam, would you and Taylor like to share our jumbo pepperoni pizza and some salad?"

"Yep! Yes. Yes. Please, do," Kate mumbled, because she was still shocked to see a TV star sitting in Bridget's living room.

Sam answered, "Well, it's our good luck that we had no plans for supper tonight. Thank you. Yes. We would love to have some pizza with you."

They all shared the pizza and salad and got to know each other. It turned out that Sam was very reserved about his fame and much more interested in how his daughter was doing in school. Did Bridget feel that Taylor was well-adjusted? Was Taylor performing well in her schoolwork?

"By the way, Bridget and Kate, do you enjoy art?" Sam asked after they had been talking for a while. "I'll be home again this weekend, and I have a friend who is an artist. He has an exhibit this weekend at a well-known art gallery downtown. I would like to repay the kindness that you have shown us: sheltering us in this terrible storm and feeding us supper. May I take you two ladies to dinner on Saturday night and to the art exhibit?"

Kate replied with a slight frown, "I'm so sorry. I cannot go this weekend, because it is my grandmother's birthday. Bridget, you should go!"

Sam looked at Bridget with a hopeful smile and said, "Well, then, Miss Bridget Cane, I would be honored if you would accompany me to dinner and an art exhibit this Saturday evening."

Bridget thought for a minute about whether it would be ethical to go out with a student's dad. Her school did not have any rules against it, so she agreed, "Okay! Thank you, Sam," she said.

"Well, it's a school night, Pumpkin," Sam said to Taylor, "and besides, I think we're keeping Miss Cane up!"

Bridget turned pink as she looked down at her robe and pajamas. "Oh, well," she said, "I'll wear something different for the art gallery. I'll wear my fancy pajamas!"

Sam, Kate, and Taylor laughed. It was a joke even a kindergartner understood. Wearing pajamas to go out on a date is funny!

After Sam and Taylor put on their raincoats and left with an umbrella that Bridget lent them, Bridget and Kate just stood there looking at each other.

"Did we just meet a TV star, Kate?" Bridget asked with a look of disbelief on her face. "This might be the most surprising, amazing thing that's happened to us in four years of teaching!"

Kate responded, "Not only did we meet a TV star, Bridget. I think you just made a date to have dinner with him this Saturday. Who will believe that you have a date with the star of 'Book and Ladder' ?"

Bridget said, "Kate, what do you mean? 'Book and Ladder'? Is that the name of his television show?"

"Yes!" squealed Kate. "He plays a guy who wants to be a writer, but he's pushed into being a fireman like his dad. So, he writes all the time when they're not fighting fires. He's writing a novel and he uses the experience he gets as a fireman. He bases his characters on the people he meets. It is a very popular TV series."

"Well," Bridget said, "I think he just wanted to ask us both out to thank us for dinner."

"Bridget, I saw the way he looked at you. He likes you!" Kate replied with a wink.

"By the way, Kate. What's this about your grandmother's birthday? Your grandmother lives in Paris!"

"Yes. She does. I just said that I had a birthday party, so that you could go out with Sam alone," Kate answered.

"Oh, Kate! You told a fib, so that I could have the handsome TV star all to myself? You ARE a good friend!" Bridget exclaimed.

Kate laughed, and then she joked, "Well, I guess I'll have a busy weekend then, flying to Paris and all!"

The two young schoolteachers giggled at each other.

As Kate approached the door to go home, she said, "Bridget, I hope you have a wonderful date with Sam on Saturday. Who knows? Maybe you'll end up in the news with the headline: TV STAR DATES BEAUTIFUL SCHOOLTEACHER."

Bridget laughed and hugged Kate. Then, she said, "You are a good friend, Kate. The next time we meet a TV star, you can date him!"

As Kate left, Bridget thought, "Wow. I'm going on a date with a TV star!"

Talking Points for "Meeting a TV Star"

- Bridget is a kindergarten teacher, and her friend Kate is a fifth-grade teacher.
- They work at the same school and have had a very exhausting day.
- Kate offered to get a pizza and bring it to Bridget's apartment for supper.
- Bridget went home to shower, throw on some comfortable pajamas, and wait for Kate.
- It began to storm and one of Bridget's students appeared on her doorstep—drenched by the rain.
- Bridget's kindergarten student, Taylor, was with her father—who is a TV star named Sam.
- As Kate arrived with the pizza, she was surprised to find a TV star and a kindergartner at Bridget's apartment.
- Owing to the terrible weather, Bridget and Kate invited Sam and Taylor to share supper with them.
- In order to thank them for sharing supper, Sam asked Bridget and Kate to have dinner with him on Saturday. He would also like to take them to an art exhibit.
- Kate constructed a fib about it being her grandmother's birthday so that Bridget would be able to go out with Sam alone.
- After Sam and his daughter left, Kate confessed her fib to Bridget.
- Bridget was excited that she had a date with a handsome TV star.

STRAIGHTFORWARD STORIES

What's Bluing?
by Virginia L. Smerglia

Lee is a sixty-four-year-old grandma. Her granddaughter, Sharon, age eight, is spending the week with her. They have just come home from a day at the zoo…so much fun! As they pitched their dirty clothes into the washing machine, Lee showed Sharon how to add the detergent and set the buttons for an extra rinse. Then, they pushed "Start."

"Did you ever help your grandmother wash clothes when you were my age, Grandma?" Sharon asked.

Lee laughed and said, "Well, it was something quite different back then. Now, we just push the buttons and we can go watch television and have some lemonade. And, Sharon, what will we do when the buzzer sounds and the washer is done?"

Sharon replied, "We'll put the clothes in the dryer and turn it on and go back to our TV movie. Maybe, we'll fold the clothes tonight or maybe we'll wait until we have time tomorrow." Then, she asked, "But how was it when you were my age, Grandma?"

Smiling, Lee explained, "Well, let me tell you about doing laundry when I was eight years old and visiting my grandma. First of all, my grandma was a homemaker. She didn't have any other job. Back then, most women worked only at home, especially if they had children, because the household chores took a lot longer. My grandma's full-time job was keeping the house and clothes clean, cooking and baking, gardening, sewing, and doing lots of other tasks for her family. However, in those days, there weren't so many machines to help. She didn't have a clothes dryer, a dishwasher, or a microwave oven. She had to make food from 'scratch.' She grew most of the vegetables and fruits and canned them for her family to eat later. But, you asked about laundry."

Lee went on, "First of all, when I was a little girl, my grandma, like most women back then, set aside certain jobs for each day of the week. She washed clothes on Monday, ironed them on Tuesday, baked on Wednesday, and cleaned the house on Thursday and Friday."

Sharon's eyes were big like saucers, and she asked. "Couldn't she ever change the days? Oh, it sounds so boring!"

Lee answered, "Well, because all the jobs took a long time and most mothers wanted to be good homemakers, they would make a schedule for themselves and try to keep it. Let me tell you about my grandma's washdays. First, laundry was always done in the basement. There were two laundry sinks together and a huge washing machine. We would gather the clothes and separate them into piles by colors. That part hasn't changed much, but everything else has. My grandma had to hang the clothes outside to dry, so we had to think about which things would take the longest to dry. We would usually wash the towels and heavy clothes first. The washing machine had two round tubs. First, we would put the clothes into the big tub and let the clothes wash awhile. Then, we would move them into the smaller tub where they would spin and the water would go out. My grandmother felt very lucky to have this kind of machine, because many women only had one with a ringer that would squeeze the water out of the clothes between two rollers. That required feeding the clothes through the ringer into the laundry sink filled with rinse water and then feeding them back through the ringer to the other laundry sink. Using a ringer washer was much more difficult! My grandma was glad that she didn't have to do that."

When Lee had explained the trouble with washing machines, Sharon added, "I guess your grandmother didn't have to work out at a gym to stay thin, Grandma! Did she?"

Lee agreed, "She sure didn't have to work out, because keeping up the house, the laundry, and the cooking was a workout all on its own! Anyhow, after we would spin the clothes, rinse them, then spin them again, and—sometimes, rinse and spin them again—we would put them in a basket and take them outside to hang up. We used clothespins to attach them to the clotheslines."

Sharon commented, "I guess you wouldn't have time to watch TV, Grandma. Would you?"

To which Lee replied, "Oh, no, Sharon! Not only was there no time to watch TV, but most homes didn't even have a TV back then! We would work straight through all morning until the clotheslines outside were full and the clothes were blowing in the wind. Then, we would eat lunch and, afterward, we would wash the lightest clothes. Those are the ones that would take the least time to dry. Oh, dear! I just realized that I forgot one step. It was called bluing."

"What's bluing?" Sharon asked.

Lee explained, "Well, ladies took a lot of pride in having very clean laundry, so they would use bleach. You know what that is. Unfortunately, clothes can become a bit yellow from using bleach to clean them. So, ladies would use a few drops from a little bottle of blue dye in order to correct the color. That dye was called bluing. I remember my grandma's apron on wash day. It was covered with blue spots!"

"Oh, dear! Grandma, it sounds like cleaning the clothes was like painting a picture. What if she added too much bluing?" Sharon asked.

"Yes. It was something that took some practice. My grandma taught me how to judge the bleaching versus the bluing, but sometimes we did make mistakes and something would turn out a bit too yellow or a bit too blue," Lee explained.

"What if it was raining, Grandma? How did you dry clothes then?" Sharon asked.

"Well, Sharon, there were two choices. We could hang the clothes in the basement to dry or switch our days around and do the baking," Lee answered.

Sharon looked at her grandmother quizzically. "Wouldn't it take a long time for clothes to dry in the basement?"

Smiling, Lee agreed, "Yes, Honey. Sometimes it took overnight, and they didn't smell fresh like when they were dried outside. Hanging clothes outside in the breeze gives them a wonderful, refreshing smell."

Sharon was enjoying hearing about her grandmother's grandma. She tried to picture her grandmother as a child. Then, after a long silence, she said, "Grandma, I guess your grandmother didn't have much time to take you to the zoo or read stories with all that work she did."

Lee got a tear in her eye as she remembered her grandmother and how she had taught her to knit and make jam and bake bread. She responded, "My grandma did take me to the zoo once, Sharon, and I remember that day like it was yesterday—even though it was so long ago. I remember my grandma and grandpa took my brother, Robby, and me to the zoo. They bought us straw Chinese hats: a blue one for my brother and a yellow one for me. They got us hotdogs, and it was a wonderful day. It was on a Saturday, when Grandma's work was done for the week. It was very unusual, and you are right that she did not have the time to do some of the things you and I might do. What was so wonderful was that she made everything we did fun—even if it was really work! I learned a lot from her, and I worked along with her. That's why I know how to take care of my garden and how to bake a lemon chiffon cake: your favorite cake! My grandma is the reason that I know how to knit your mittens. She taught me how to do it, and she loved me and spent time with me. That part hasn't changed, Sharon. Grandmothers still love their grandchildren and enjoy spending time with them."

Sharon smiled. Then, she frowned a little bit and said, "Grandma, there's something I don't think I'd like about how the laundry was done when you were a little girl."

Lee asked, "What's that, Honey? The time it took?"

Sharon responded, "No, Grandma, I think if that was what everyone did and there were no dryers, then we'd just be used to it. But, I don't think I'd like hanging my underwear out in the yard for everyone to see!" At the thought of it, Sharon blushed.

Lee chuckled and said, "What my grandma taught me, Sharon, was to hang the underwear on a line between the sheets and the towels so the neighbors wouldn't see it!"

Talking Points for "What's Bluing?"

- Lee is sixty-four years old and her granddaughter, Sharon, is eight.
- They are spending the day together.
- They went to the zoo. When they got home, they decided to wash their dirty clothes.
- As Lee showed Sharon how to do the laundry, she explained how different it was back when she was a child.
- Lee told Sharon about her own grandmother and how she taught her many things, like how to do laundry, how to cook and bake, and how to knit.
- Back when Lee was a child, her grandmother had a large washing machine that was two tubs. They would wash the clothes in one, then spin them in the other. After that, they would put them back in the first tub to rinse them. Finally, they would spin them again.
- Washing clothes was very hard work when Lee was young.
- She explained to Sharon that bleach was used in the laundry, and people would use "bluing" in order to keep the clothes from becoming too yellow.
- People would hang the laundry out on the clothesline with clothespins.
- Sharon enjoyed hearing about her grandmother as a child, but she was worried about having to hang her underwear outside on the clothesline for everyone to see.
- Lee told her about a trick: to hang the underwear on a line in the middle—between two other clotheslines with sheets and towels on them. That way people wouldn't be able to see the delicate items.

Lots Of Things Happen In Pittsburgh In The Rain!
by Virginia L. Smerglia

It was a rainy Friday in Pittsburgh, Pennsylvania. It was the last Friday in July, and it was raining very hard. It was a rain storm! The raindrops were hitting windows so hard that people could barely hear.

Anyone who has been to Pittsburgh knows it is a very hilly place. Most people live in houses and apartments on hillsides. People have to park their cars on hillsides. Gardens are planted on all kinds of slopes. Pretty much everything that happens in Pittsburgh happens somewhere on a hill. The only flat place is Downtown Pittsburgh with its skyscrapers and parks by the rivers.

Because of the hills, a rainstorm in Pittsburgh can be an event! If the weather has been dry for a week or so, the streets become slippery just like icy streets. Then, cars slide around and bump into each other. Great streams of water pour through hillside gardens, carrying away soil and seed and leaving ditches. In city neighborhoods, children make paper boats and sail them down the gutters. In the suburbs, people build walls of brick and stone to keep their lawns from slipping away.

On this particular stormy Friday in Pittsburgh, quite a few people were preparing for the wedding of a girl named Tina and her fiancé, Jeff. The wedding was to be in the evening: a beautiful summer wedding. And, it was to be, you guessed it, at a church on a hillside. Actually, the wedding was to be in the church's gardens. Oh, dear! The bride and groom were getting upset as the rain continued all afternoon. Tina and Jeff and their parents had been talking on the phone all day.

Tina sat looking out the window, crying. "My garden wedding is ruined," she said to her mother.

Wanting to do something to help, Tina's mother decided to go see the church gardens herself. "The church is six miles away," she said. "Maybe it's just sprinkling there, Tina."

Tina's mom covered her hair—which was all styled for the wedding—got a big golf umbrella from the garage, and drove to the church. When she got there, the florists were sitting in their van looking gloomy. The van was filled with baskets of beautiful sunflowers. Those were about the only sunny things in Pittsburgh on that day! The pastor was standing at the church door talking to some people who were waiting to set up rented tables and chairs. The caterers were putting up a tent to cover their barbecue grills and coolers of food. As all this was going on, mud was running down the hillside, through the church gardens and out onto the parking lot.

Tina's mom tried to calm herself as she approached the church door. She said, "Pastor Stein, what can we do? The gardens are filled with muddy water, and we have two hundred wedding guests coming. The church will never hold that many people."

The pastor said, "Now, Darlene, let's just say a small prayer." He took her hand, bowed his head, and started to pray before Darlene could say anything. "Lord, we trust you. Please show us a solution to this problem of so much rain. Right now, we can't see any way to hold Tina and Jeff's wedding. Please, help us to find a solution. Amen."

Just then, the people with a truck full of rental chairs and tables came over and said, "This is a terrible day for us. Not only is there mud where your wedding is supposed to be, but we just got a call from the mall that their indoor garden exhibit and dinner have been cancelled, because not enough people made reservations. Now, we have no chair deliveries to make…anywhere!"

Reverend Stein and Darlene looked at each other, and Reverend Stein asked, "Are you talking about the new mall?"

"Yes. You know…it's about three and a half miles from here," answered the chair delivery man.

Thinking fast, Darlene asked, "Can you get the mall manager back on your cell phone?"

And, so it was, that on a stormy Friday night in Pittsburgh, Pennsylvania, a bride named Tina and her groom, Jeff, were married in the center of a garden exhibit in the middle of the new shopping mall. Not only were there sunflowers, but there were beautiful gardens with special twinkling lights and hanging baskets of ivy and blue delphiniums. There were park benches and lovely ponds with orange and silvery fish.

In the midst of this, the chair people had set up tables around which were seated two hundred wedding guests. The caterers were carrying trays of food in and out of the mall's huge new kitchen. The children were feeding bread crumbs to the fish in the ponds. If people had looked up, they would have seen the rain drumming down on the glass roof of the new mall, but no one did look up. And, probably, the bride and groom will never forget how blessed they were to have a rain storm in Pittsburgh on their wedding day on that last Friday in July. If it had been sunny outside, they never would have had a wedding with indoor gardens, fish ponds, fountains, and park benches, and they wouldn't have heard shoppers applauding as they said, "I do!" Most of all, they wouldn't have had the most unique wedding of the year, with guests dancing under twinkling lights and in front of colorful shop windows! For all their married lives, Tina and Jeff had a wonderful story to tell about their wedding day.

Talking Points for "Lots Of Things Happen In Pittsburgh In The Rain!"

- Pittsburgh, Pennsylvania is a very hilly city.
- Except for the downtown area, Pittsburgh is built on hills, and when it rains, things get interesting!
- Rain runs down streets and through people's yards—carrying mud and people's lawns, too! Children make sailboats to float down the rushing water in the gutters.
- On a very rainy Friday in July, Tina and Jeff's beautiful garden wedding seemed unlikely to take place.
- The garden of the church had flooded.
- In the midst of this dilemma, Tina's mom discovered that a garden exhibit and dinner at the new shopping mall had been cancelled.
- Tina's mom thought fast and arranged to have the wedding moved indoors to the shopping mall.
- Tina and Jeff were married amid beautiful twinkling lights, fish ponds, fountains, and lovely flowers as shoppers looked on, and the wedding guests enjoyed being inside, rather than out in the pouring rain!

Feeding The Ducks
by Lauren Smerglia Seifert

For almost as long as they had been sisters, Nettie and Grace had walked to Memorial Park each week. They liked to go to the pond and feed the ducks, and they helped out in the park by picking up litter and placing it in trash bins.

It was Sunday afternoon again, and the two ladies were strolling arm-in-arm along the sidewalk toward the pond. This was their time—"sister time"—when they could share their hopes and dreams with each other. Once, Nettie had seen a sign in a café that stated: "WHO NEEDS A THERAPIST WHEN YOU HAVE A SISTER?" They had both laughed about it, because it seemed very true for them.

The two sisters had been taking their Sunday walks together since just after Nettie's third birthday. It had been a hot July day, and seven-year-old Grace had asked whether they could go to the park. Their mother had agreed, and Mom had followed behind while Nettie and Grace held hands and skipped along in front of her. That had been the first of many Sunday afternoons when they would enjoy their time together at Memorial Park. Nowadays, as retired schoolteachers, Nettie and Grace usually took longer walks, because they wanted to stay healthy. Also, the fresh air brightened their spirits and refreshed their minds.

On this Sunday in June, it was especially breezy. Nettie had worn her straw hat, but the wind kept trying to pick it up off her head! Thus, as they walked along, Nettie had one arm tucked against her sister's, and the other arm was holding her hat on.

"It is such a blustery day today! It seems more like September than early June," Grace remarked.

Nettie replied, "Yes, my dear. It most certainly is breezy!"

As they reached Memorial Park, the wind caught the brim of Nettie's hat and she struggled to hold it on her head. Grace suggested that she take the hat off and put it in her bag, and so she did. However, as the two ladies gathered litter and placed it in garbage cans in the park, the sun was hot—even with the wind gusts. So, Nettie decided to put her hat back on, because she was afraid that she would get sunburned.

"Oh, dear, Grace," Nettie called. "I don't know what to do. The sun is so bright that I need my hat. Otherwise, my cheeks will turn red! How will I keep my hat from blowing away?"

Her big sister came to the rescue, suggesting a hair clip. Grace removed a hair clip from her own hair and used it to fasten Nettie's straw hat to the front of her hair.

"There!" Grace exclaimed. "Now, your hat will stay on your head, and you won't get sunburned."

As the two sisters finished gathering litter from the grass in Memorial Park, they put the last few pieces of paper in a nearby garbage bin. Then, they turned toward the duck pond. It had been a very wet springtime, and the new ducklings were just starting to wander out of the nesting area. Grace and Nettie loved to bring a bag of old bread and feed the ducks. Today, they decided to sit on a bench and throw pieces of stale Italian bread into the water. As usual, the adult ducks quacked and squawked at one another—each trying to get the most bread for itself.

    It was funny to see that the new ducklings were wandering around in the grass near the pond. They were not paying attention to the goings-on in the water. One specific duckling caught Grace's eye. It was bending down to investigate something in the grass.

    "Look, Nettie!" laughed Grace. "Look at the darling duckling!"

    Just as Nettie turned her attention toward the duckling, her hair clip came loose, a gust of wind caught her hat, and the hat blew toward the little duck. Now, this straw hat had a very wide brim. It was no small hat! As the hat blew to the ground, it started rolling. It skimmed along the ground, right toward the tiny duck!

"Quack! Quack!" called the duckling as it saw the large hat rolling toward it.

"Oh, no, Grace! My hat is going to hit the duckling!" Nettie called, panicked that her broad-brimmed straw hat would hurt the baby duck.

Luckily, as the hat rolled, it came to rest in the grass with the inside up. So, the hat almost looked like a giant tea cup resting in the grass.

"Oh, thank goodness!" Nettie sighed. "I'm so glad my hat didn't hit that little duckling."

Nettie and Grace got up from the bench and started walking toward Nettie's straw hat—which was now resting upside-down in the grass, but what happened next was something that nobody could have predicted. Before the two sisters reached the hat, the little duckling waddled clumsily up to it and…

JUMPED INTO THE HAT!

That's right. Nettie's hat was now in the grass—with a tiny duck sitting right in it.

"What should we do?" Nettie asked her sister.

"Oh, it's simple, dear," responded Grace. "We'll just dump the little guy out onto the grass, so that we can retrieve your hat."

It seemed like good advice that Nettie had received from her big sister. However, when Nettie reached down to grasp the brim of the straw hat, the little duck who was sitting in it snapped at her hand—just missing her pinky finger! Then, the duck squawked and quacked. Clearly, the duck wanted the hat.

A bit afraid of the duckling and whether it might bite her, Nettie suggested that she and Grace sit back down on the bench. Surely, they said to each other, the duckling would tire of the hat and wander off soon. Alas! Two hours later, after several attempts to dump the duckling out of the straw hat, they were no closer to having the hat back again!

As the dinner hour approached, Nettie's stomach growled. She thought about eating some of the stale bread crumbs that they had brought along for feeding the ducks, but all the bits of bread were already gone. As Nettie's stomach growled even louder, her big sister suggested that they should be going.

Grace said, "Let's leave the hat for the little duck. I'm hungry and it's supper time. Besides, Honey, you can always get another hat."

Nettie frowned and replied, "Okay. Since I cannot seem to coax the little duck away from my hat, I guess we'll have to let him have it."

As the two ladies walked arm-in-arm away from the park, they were both thinking about how hungry they were for supper. It had been quite an afternoon of picking up litter, feeding the ducks, and trying to get Nettie's hat back from the little duckling!

"You know, Nettie. I've always thought that straw hat was too big for you, anyway. It made your head look too small!" Grace said with a grin as the two ladies walked away from the park.

After that day, and during all of that summer, whenever Grace and Nettie would walk to Memorial Park, they would see that little duck, and no matter how faded and dirty Nettie's old straw hat got, the duck was always sitting in it!

Talking Points for "Feeding The Ducks"

- Nettie and Grace are sisters who walk in Memorial Park each week.
- One Sunday in early June, the two sisters walked in the park and picked up litter.
- Nettie wore a hat with a broad brim in order to protect herself from the sun.
- It was windy, so Grace took one of her own hair clips and tried to fasten Nettie's hat so that it wouldn't blow away.
- Even so, Nettie's hat did blow away when the two sisters were feeding the ducks.
- A tiny duck took an interest in Nettie's hat—which had landed near him in the grass.
- The duckling jumped into Nettie's hat and would not give it up!
- After two hours, Nettie and Grace decided to let the little duck have the straw hat.
- All summer long, whenever Nettie and Grace walked to the park, they would find that little duck sitting in the straw hat.

The Climbing Tree
by Virginia L. Smerglia

There was a climbing tree in the woods behind my house when I was a little girl. My brother and I and all the kids in our neighborhood used to climb it just about every day. It had branches about every eighteen inches. The spacing of the branches made it easy to climb all the way to the top. It was a tall tree, and it was a long way to the top!

The first branch was only about two feet off the ground, so that even little children could climb up a couple of limbs. Usually, kids in our neighborhood would start there at the bottom and as we grew, we'd go higher. On any given summer day, the tree would be filled with kids, with little four- and five-year-olds at the bottom, eleven- or twelve-year-olds at the top, and everyone else spread out in-between.

You may think kids would climb up the tree, come down the tree, and then go do something else. That wasn't the way our climbing tree worked. We would stay in that tree for hours! On some days, the tree would be a place for heroes. The oldest kid at the top would be someone like Superman®, and we would concoct exciting adventures about how Superman® would save the world!

Sometimes, the tree was our castle. We tied ropes to the longest branches. We would divide into two groups and take turns defending the castle from "bad guys." We would swing down on the ropes to take the pretend invaders by surprise.

If older kids were playing, the tree would be an office building and the person on the top branch would be the "boss" who ordered us all around. We weren't sure exactly what bosses did, but we all knew from our parents that a boss is someone who gives orders! So, the boss at the top of the tree would give orders, and the rest of us would follow along.

In May, when wild apple trees in the woods were filled with fragrant pink and white blossoms, we would pick branches of blossoms and put them in our climbing tree as decorations. If just the girls were playing, we'd have a make-believe wedding. Once in awhile, some of the boys would agree to be part of the wedding and would play the roles of the groom and the minister or priest. Don't ask how a wedding could be in a tree. When children are imagining, anything is possible!

In July, we'd put American flags in the tree and pretend it was a float in a big Fourth of July parade. If we were decorating our bikes for the real parade, we'd use some of the leftover crepe paper to make streamers and drape the tree with them.

In autumn, the leaves of our tree turned scarlet red. It was an oak tree, you see, and maybe the most beautiful tree of all! In the fall, we could climb up into the tree, look out to view all the woods around us, and see the many colors. As leaves fell, we could look further and further into the woods, and the games we played would change. For one thing, the days were getting shorter, there was homework to do, and there were after-school activities. After school started in the fall, we had to invent short games. We didn't have the luxury of time. The time we did have for climbing and imagining was precious, because we knew the long days of summer were not to come again for quite awhile.

In winter, a shallow pond would form around the tree and freeze. The ice would last through most of January and February. The water froze around the tree and made an ice skating pond. We'd skate in our ice skates or slide around in our boots. We would circle the tree, grabbing the lower branches and pulling ourselves from one to another.

We were always sad when, usually early in March, the ice began to crack. That meant the end of great fun, but before the ice melted completely, we would jump on it and crack it just for the fun of hearing the sound. Since the water was only about ten inches deep, we could stomp around, float on the big pieces of ice, pick them up and make a pile out of them, or do whatever else came to mind. It was such fun! One winter afternoon, our mother was upset with us, because we got our clothes soaking wet with the icy water from around the tree. She was sure we'd catch pneumonia, but we did not. Thank, goodness!

My brother and I lived in the house with the climbing tree for eleven years. By the time we moved, I was a fourteen-year-old girl: too old for tree-climbing. My brother was almost at the end of his climbing years, as well. I always think of that tree in a good way and remember all the happy hours and days spent in and around it. In all of that time, there was never a child who fell out of the tree. There was never a child who got more than a minor scrape from it. No one even got poison ivy! I don't remember any parent telling us to get down from the tree—unless it was dinner time.

Now that I look back on it, I don't think we realized how special that tree was. It was just a part of our neighborhood. Thinking back, I believe it was a very wonderful gift in my childhood, and I often wonder about the children who enjoyed it after we moved away. I hope they had fun in it, too.

Talking Points for "The Climbing Tree"

- When I was growing up, I lived in a house that had a wonderful climbing tree in the yard.
- My brother and I and all the kids in the neighborhood spent many hours climbing that oak tree.
- We would imagine the tree was a castle, and we would defend it from invaders.
- Sometimes, the kids would pretend that the tree was an office building, and one of the big kids would be the "boss."
- We, girls, would decorate the tree with apple blossoms and have pretend weddings in it.
- In autumn, the tree turned scarlet red, and we would climb it to look out over all the pretty colors of fall.
- In winter, water froze around the base of the tree—making a pond. We would skate around on it, or slide around in our boots.
- In the spring, we would break up the ice. One time, we got completely soaking wet, and my mom thought my brother and I would get sick, but we didn't. Thank, goodness!
- Over the years, nobody ever got hurt in the tree and no one ever got poison ivy.
- It was a wonderful part of my childhood, and I hope that many more kids enjoyed the climbing tree after we moved away.

STRAIGHTFORWARD STORIES

The following version of "The Mailman's Mystery" is different than the one presented in Chapter 2. This one is simpler and written to suit persons with moderate-to-severe neurocognitive impairment/dementia.

The Mailman's Mystery
by Virginia L. Smerglia and Lauren Smerglia Seifert

This story takes place in downtown Cleveland. It is about a mailman named Wilson and some mysterious events which occurred on his mail route. People call Wilson a "mailman," but as Wilson will tell you, he likes to be called a "postal carrier" or a "mail carrier."

As you can imagine, since his route is in downtown Cleveland, most of his customers are in business offices. He delivers mail to the offices of doctors, dentists, lawyers, accountants, financial advisors, and even some companies. Many people know him because he goes into the offices with his big mail bags, and he is usually met by the workers assigned to receive the mail.

Wilson's route is actually only one building. It has forty-five floors and many offices on each floor. Because the building has so many offices, it takes Wilson all day to deliver the mail. He has a cart to transport the mail bags, and he uses the service elevators.

One sunny Tuesday morning in June, Wilson was in high spirits as he started his mail deliveries, because he and his brother were going to see the Cleveland Indians play that night. He was imagining those great stadium hotdogs, some cold beer, popcorn, and perfect weather. His favorite pitcher was on the mound that night and he wanted to be sure to be there for the first pitch. He was making good time going in and out of offices and greeting everyone with a smile. Wilson was telling people that he was going to attend the baseball game that evening. When he got to the ninth floor, he left his cart in the hall and carried the heavy mailbag into a doctor's office. He stopped to chitchat with Carol, the receptionist, because he knew she was an Indians fan.

When Wilson came out into the hall and started to move his cart, there on top of his sacks of mail sat a monkey. That's right! Wilson saw a very little monkey sitting on top of his mail cart. Wilson could not believe his eyes! A cute little monkey was sitting on his mail cart! But how did a monkey get into a building in the middle of downtown Cleveland?

Wilson went back into the doctor's office and asked Carol whether anybody had reported a missing monkey.

"A what?" Carol asked and laughed.

Page 119

"Truly!" Wilson replied. "There is a little monkey sitting on my mail cart out in the hallway."

Wilson used Carol's phone to call his boss and report the situation. Then Wilson and Carol walked back out to his cart in the hallway, but [surprise!] there was no monkey! Carol thought maybe Wilson was playing a joke on her, but he assured her that the monkey was real. After Wilson and Carol looked around for the monkey, they both had to get back to work. Carol went back into her office, and Wilson went back to making his mail deliveries.

After work, Wilson met his brother at the stadium and watched an exciting baseball game. The Indians won by one run in the ninth inning! It was a warm summer evening. There was lots of good food to eat, and Wilson did not think about the little monkey again.

The next day, Wilson went about his mail delivery route as usual. When he got to the ninth floor, he looked around for the monkey, but did not see anything. He talked to Carol about the Indians' exciting win. As he left, Wilson asked her if there was any news about the monkey.

Carol answered, "No. The building was searched, but nothing was found."

Wilson continued his delivery route. When he came back to his cart from an office on the twelfth floor—[guess what?]—there again was the little monkey sitting—as pretty as you please—on top of his mail cart. This time, the monkey was eating an oatmeal cookie!

Taking no chances, Wilson called his supervisor. In a few minutes, two elevators opened at the same time and as the supervisor stepped off one elevator, the monkey jumped onto the other elevator—and the doors closed. Wilson and his boss tried to catch the monkey, but it was just too fast!

Now, there was a mystery, and there was a little monkey in the office building! Wilson's supervisor asked him if he had any idea why the monkey kept going to his mail cart, but he didn't know why. He had lost so much time over the monkey that he needed to get back to his mail deliveries.

Needless to say, on the next day, which was Thursday, Wilson wondered whether the cute little monkey would reappear. He had told his family and some of his friends about the animal. None of them knew anyone with a pet monkey. Wilson was relieved when Thursday came and went with no more sightings of the monkey and, by the end of the day, Wilson figured the monkey had gone back to wherever he was from.

Friday morning dawned hot and humid in Cleveland. It was predicted to be 96 degrees! Wilson was looking forward to the weekend. He was planning to go swimming and picnicking with his brother's family on Saturday. He was also hoping to watch the Indians on TV on Sunday. He tried never to miss a game!

As he went about his rounds, Wilson saw Carol and they talked about Sunday afternoon's double-header and the Indians' chances. He kept up a good pace and was on the forty-fifth floor. He had to carry two big bags of mail into an attorney's office, and it was hot. Wilson was wiping his brow, glad the day was almost over, when he came out of the attorney's office. Then, as he walked toward his mail cart—[Oh, no! You guessed it!]—there sat the monkey, right on top of the mail cart!

Now, Wilson was tempted to try to grab the little monkey, but the zoo had told his boss that he and Wilson should not try to touch the monkey. They should just try to keep it on one floor and call the animal rescue workers, who are sometimes called "dog catchers." Thinking about this, Wilson called the animal rescue emergency number and called his boss again.

While he waited for his boss to arrive, Wilson noticed that the little monkey had jumped off the mail cart and was running down the hallway. Wilson followed it, and soon the monkey ran into an office at the end of the hallway.

      Wilson decided to go into that office. He opened the door and walked in…and what do you think? Inside the office was a nicely dressed lady at a desk, and she was just typing away. And what do you think was perched on her shoulder? You guessed it! The little monkey was sitting up on the nice lady's right shoulder! And that monkey was just as still as a statue and it was staring right at Wilson!

      As Wilson walked toward the lady's desk, she looked up and asked, "May I help you, Sir?"

      Wilson, stood there. He looked at the little monkey and, then, he looked at the lady. He said, "The monkey. The monkey. I've been seein' him all week long!"

      The lady replied, "Well of course you have, dear. This little one doesn't like to wait for his mail, and it seems that you always start at the ground floor and work your way up. So, he has to wait all day long for his mail, and he isn't a very patient fellow!"

      And that is the story about the little monkey in an office on the forty-fifth floor of the building where Wilson delivered mail. He was a monkey who didn't like to wait all day long for his mail! So, he went to the mail cart to get it.

Talking Points for "The Mailman's Mystery"

- Wilson is a mailman who works in Cleveland, Ohio.
- His entire mail route is in a forty-five-story office building.
- One day, while Wilson was thinking about the upcoming Cleveland Indians' baseball game, he found a little monkey sitting on top of his mail cart.
- Before Wilson's boss arrived to help, the monkey disappeared.
- That night, Wilson had fun with his brother at the baseball game, and the Indians won!
- The next day, while Wilson was delivering mail, he found the monkey sitting on his mail cart again.
- Then, on Friday of the same week, when Wilson was almost done delivering the mail, the monkey appeared again!
- Wilson called the animal rescue workers and his boss.
- He followed the monkey down a hallway and into an office where a nice lady sat at her desk typing.
- The monkey had perched on the lady's shoulder and was staring at Wilson.
- When Wilson asked the lady about the monkey, she replied very politely that the monkey doesn't like to wait all day long to get his mail. That's why he comes to the mail cart to get it!

The 5 Big Hints

The 5 Big Hints task is especially designed for groups who have members with cognitive decline—especially those with Alzheimer's disease (AD). One can find the full instructions to 5 Big Hints at www.clovepress.com. Many more "5 Big Hints" examples can be found in *Roses Grow in a Butterfly Garden*, without photo images. Also, 50 pre-made (8.5" X 5.5") cards with the hints and photos can be purchased at www.clovepress.com.

The instructions herein are not intended as specific consultation. Individual professionals are responsible for assessing their appropriateness for application.

It is typical to present 10 to 20 items in a 30 – 60 minute activity session. The goal is to provide memory cueing in ways that are informed by scientific research on memory loss (as discussed in the book *Roses Grow in a Butterfly Garden*, available at www.clovepress.com).

"5 Big Hints" is designed very specifically to aid remembering in AD and related types of dementia. The cues are tailored to help participants guess the target item. <u>Present the items and their hints one-at-a-time.</u>

Give Category: Present Hint #2:   Present Hint #3:   Present Hint #4:
And then Present Hint #5:

Giving Hints: Speak and Print
Provide each hint in the game verbally and in print. Start the session by printing the terms, "5 Big Hints"; "Category"; and "Hint # __" in erasable, large black or navy print down the left side of a whiteboard (in a column). Then, use another color (e.g., dark green on a whiteboard) to fill in the actual hints for an item during a round (e.g., "ANIMAL"; "It lives in the water."). The different colors of ink help to define the two columns (left v. right). The terms on the left side of the board (like "Category") stay in place from round to round, but the words on the right side (i.e., the specific hints) are erased after each round.

Use all CAPITAL letters for printing the category label. Other labels and hints are printed in upper- and lower-cases, with no cursive writing. Try to keep the sentences simple, so that complicated grammar doesn't confuse lower-functioning participants. Also, about the whiteboard, do not use red ink. It makes the letters harder to see.

TELMIA

It is best to begin with a category clue (e.g., animal, location, transportation/vehicle, etc.). Thus, "Category" is the first hint. Usually, the fifth hint is an aesthetically pleasing picture of the target item, or you might show a picture of the item *immediately* after Hint #5. Show the picture, regardless of whether the participants have guessed its name correctly during the previous hints, because the picture serves as a visual cue to aid memory and to reward participants.

Generally, an activity session with "5 Big Hints" has 10 – 15 participants, whose seats are arranged in auditorium-style. However, this task can work one-on-one or with small groups (up to 5). The cards to accompany these instructions carry clues on one side and an item's picture on the reverse side. If using the two-sided cards from Clove Press LTD, keep the picture facing down while reading the hints. That way, participants won't accidentally see the picture before the last hint for it is given!

A mixed group (with both high- and lower-functioning participants) will not work well if some of the higher-functioning members are prone to impatience. It is fruitful to know who might enjoy taking part and to select personalities that will "gel well" rather than "grind like metal on metal!" Playing competitively (in teams) can work, if it suits participants' personalities.

To make the activity suitable for a mixture of cognitive levels, include some easier items and some more difficult ones. Showing a picture at the end of each round helps to provide cognitive stimulation and pleasure for all participants—regardless of whether they guessed correctly during that round or not. It's important that pictures have artistic qualities, and that they do not merely look like photos taken from a grade-school picture book. The artistic quality of the pictures adds to enjoyment of the activity.

With respect to the order of stimuli (pictures), do not use two items from the same category in consecutive order. Especially for persons with Alzheimer-type dementia, the problem of perseveration is common. It can lead a person to think of and name the same item several times in succession. Given this phenomenon in AD, it can create undesirable interference in memory when one item from a category is presented right after another item from the same category. It might lead a person to continue to say the name of the just-previously-presented exemplar. This is the reason that the hints (in Dr. Seifert's book, *Roses Grow in a Butterfly Garden*) are not arranged by category. Do rearrange their sequencing from session-to-session and week-to-week, in an effort to provide variety, but maintain the rule that consecutive items are not from the same category.

Category: ANIMAL

Hint #2: It is a type of INSECT.

Hint #3: It comes out of a cocoon.

Hint #4: It has pretty wings.

Hint #5: It starts with the sound, "B" [saying, "buh", rather than the letter name].

Butterfly

TELMIA

Page 126

FIVE BIG HINTS

Category: BUILDING

Hint #2: It is a tall building.

Hint #3: It is usually on a beach or waterfront.

Hint #4: It is used to signal ships.

Hint #5: This building shines a bright light at night and during storms.

Lighthouse

TELMIA

Category: ANIMAL

Hint #2: It is a large BIRD.

Hint #3: It has a very brightly colored, blue and green tail.

Hint #4: It "struts" to show the lady birds its tail.

Hint #5: "As proud as a _____."

Peacock

TELMIA

Category: BUILDING

Hint #2: It is a government building.

Hint #3: It is in Washington, D.C.

Hint #4: It has a dome on it.

Hint #5: It is white.

The U.S. Capitol Building

TELMIA

Category: PLANT

Hint #2: It is a large FLOWER.

Hint #3: It grows during harvest.

Hint #4: It is yellow, with a brown center.

Hint #5: It is TALL.
[Additionally, people love to roast and eat this flower's seeds.]

Sunflower

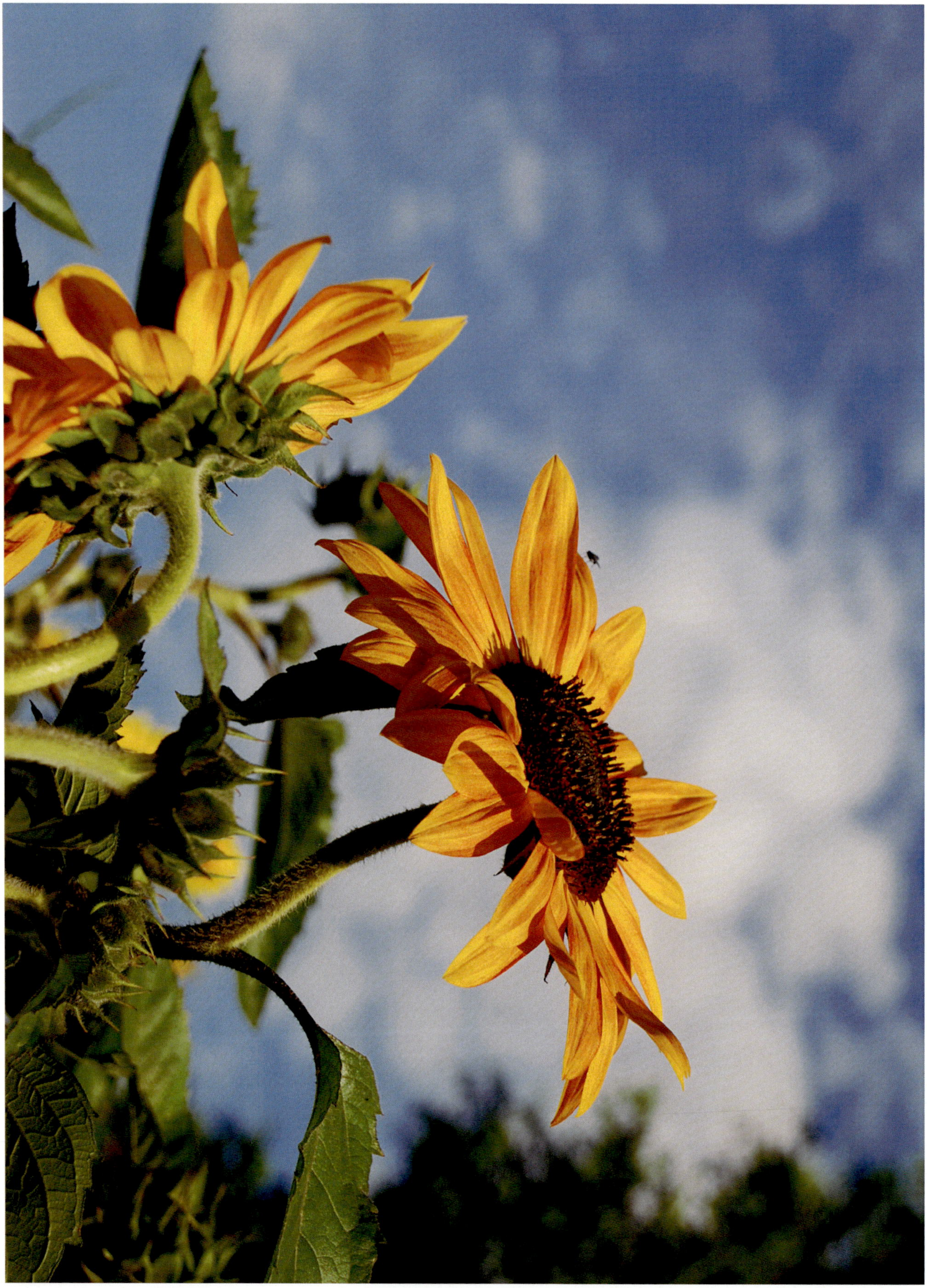

Category: ANIMAL

Hint #2: It has four legs.

Hint #3: It has a mane.

Hint #4: It is 'the king of the jungle!'

Hint #5: Its name starts with "L" (saying "luh" rather than the letter's name).

Lion

TELMIA

Category: TRANSPORTATION/VEHICLE

Hint #2: It runs on tracks (or rails).

Hint #3: It can haul cargo over long distances.

Hint #4: Its engine can be driven by steam or coal.

Hint #5: It is a freight _____.

Train

TELMIA

Category: FOOD

Hint #2: This food is Italian.

Hint #3: It has a crust with tomato sauce and cheese on it.

Hint #4: Some people like thin crust, while others like thick.

Hint #5: "I'd like some pepperoni _____."

Pizza

TELMIA

Category: TRANSPORTATION/VEHICLE

Hint #2: It travels on water.

Hint #3: It is important to have wind, or this vehicle won't go very far!

Hint #4: It has a mast.

Hint #5: The captain might say, "Unfurl the main sail!"

Sailboat

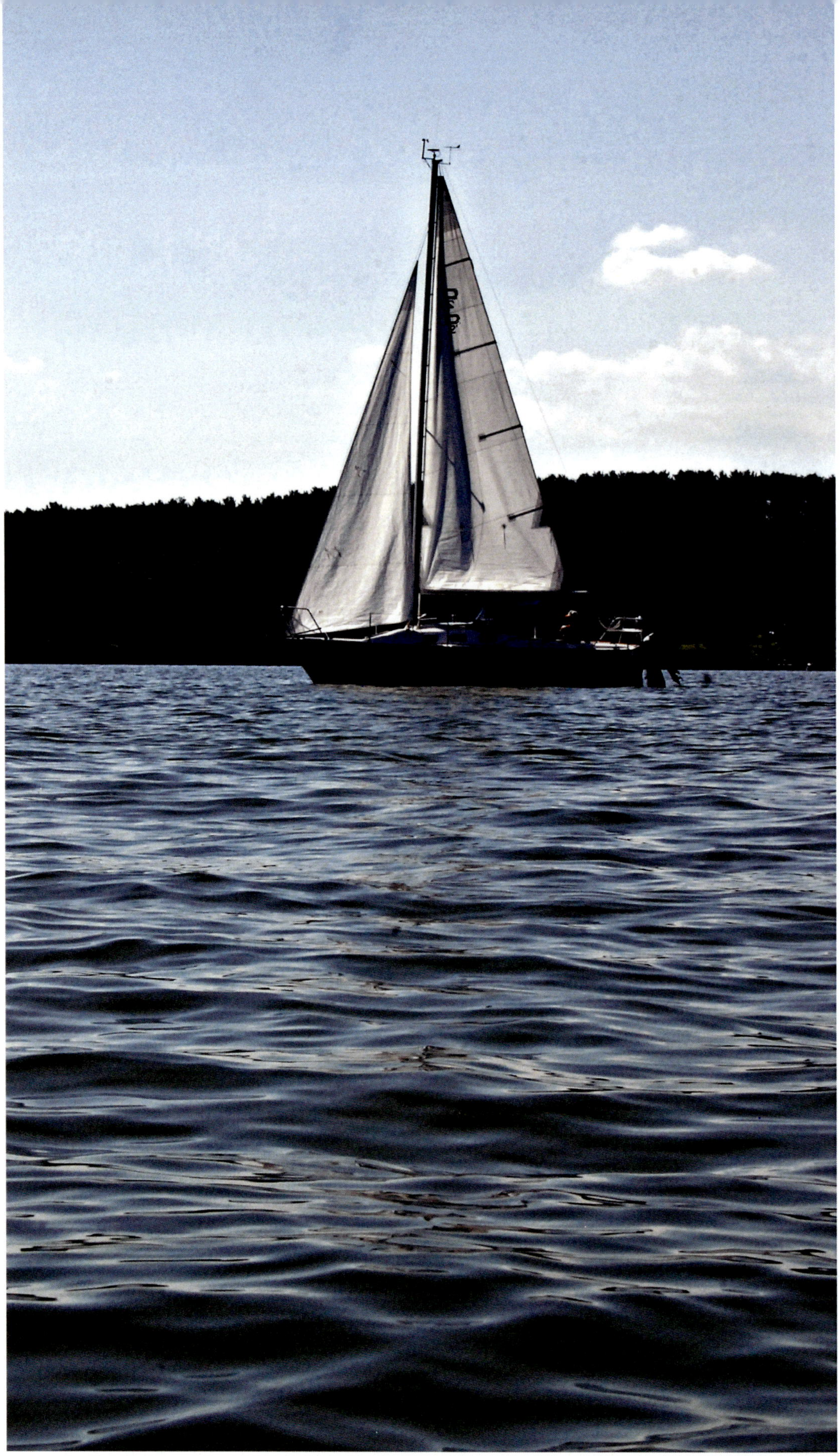

Category: ANIMAL

Hint #2: It is a type of FISH.

Hint #3: Some people like to put them in an aquarium.

Hint #4: This type of fish is so pretty, that it is named after heavenly beings that have wings.

Hint #5: On a vacation to the Tropics, you might go snorkeling and see this.

Angelfish

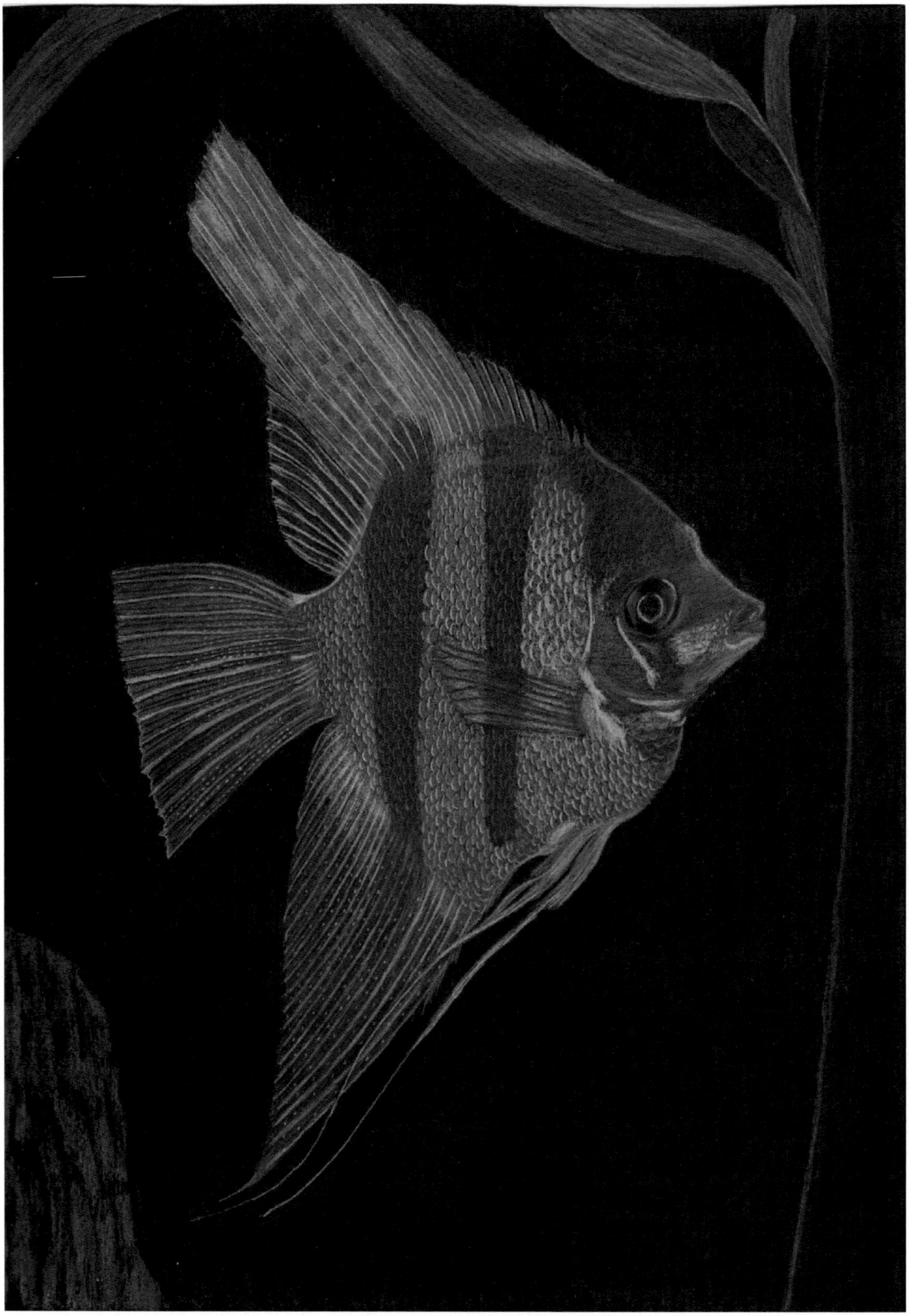

Appendix

Infusing Interventions into Individualized Care:
A Hierarchy of Goals
[A View of Greenspan and Wieder's (1998) 'Integrated Intervention':
Adapted to eldercare by Seifert (2007)]

Lauren has put together these intervention goals and listed them in her previous books. This time around they are listed from first-through-fifth. Therefore, they are like steps. Ideally, person-centered care happens at all levels all the time!

Person-centered, integrated care includes the following:

1) support for medical/physical care and consideration of environment
For example, through regular check-ups and attention to medications and physical changes, with care given to physical context and physiological functions

2) structure for integrity in relationships
For example, addressing individuals by name, in caring tones, and without "baby-talk"

3) interactions to accentuate personal abilities and needs for sensing stimuli, interpreting incoming information, and planning actions
For example, with a variety of activity choices—some active and some passive—like reading aloud v. listening to someone else read

4) intervention strategies that promote independence and support one's current level of functioning
For example, fostering autonomy by providing options and allowing a person some freedom to make choices (like meal times and food selections)

5) person-centered interventions that are motivated by the specific history, preferences, and personality of the individual AND support to transcend/transform in context, when/if possible
For example, helping an artist with AD demonstrate brushwork to a small group of art students, or reading aloud together with a retired pre-school teacher

General References

American Psychiatric Association. (2001). *Diagnostic and statistical manual of mental disorders* (4th ed., text revised). Washington, DC: Author.

American Psychatric Association. (2011). *Information about the DSM-5*. Retrieved from http://www.DSM5.org

Antonucci, T.C., Tamir, L., & Dubnoff, S. (1980). Mental health across the family life cycle. In K.W. Black (Ed.), *Life course: Integrative theories and exemplary populations.* Boulder, CO: Westview Press.

Arking, R. (1991). *Biology of aging: Observations and principles.* Englewood Cliff, NJ: Prentice-Hall.

Baker, M.K., & Seifert, L.S. (2007, August). Maintenance of cognitive skills in persons with Alzheimer-type dementia. Poster presented at the 115th annual meeting of the American Psychological Association, San Francisco, CA.

Baltes, P.B., & Lindenberger, U. (1997). Emergence of a powerful connection between sensory and cognitive functions across the adult life span: A new window to the study of cognitive aging? *Psychology and Aging, 12,* 12-21.

Bergman, M. (1971). Hearing and aging: Implications of recent research findings. *Audiology, 10,* 164-171.

Bjorklund, B.R. (2011). *The journey of adulthood* (7th ed.). Boston, MA: Prentice Hall.

Deary, I.J., Weiss, A., & Batty, G.D. (2010, August). Intelligence, personality, and health outcomes. *Psychological Science in the Public Interest, 11*(2), 53-79.

Doty, R.L., Shaman, P., Applebaum, S.C., Giberson, R., Sikorski, L., & Rosenberg, L. (1984, December 21). Smell identification ability: Changes with age. *Science, 226* (4681), 1441-1443. Retrieved from: http://www.jstor.org/stable/1693918

Ebbinghaus, H. (1885/1964). *Memory: A contribution to experimental psychology.* New York: Dover Publications. (Trans. H.A. Ruger, C.E. Bussenius, with E.R. Hilgard).

REFERENCES

Folstein, M.F., Folstein, S.E., & McHugh, P.R. (1975). 'Mini-Mental State': A practical method for grading the cognitive states of patients for the clinician. *Journal of Psychiatric Research, 12,* 196-198.

Foos, P.W., & Clark, M.C. (2008). *Human aging* (2nd ed.). Boston, MA: Pearson Education.

Greenspan, S.J., & Wieder, S. (1998). *The child with special needs: Encouraging intellectual and emotional growth.* (with contributions from Robin Simons). Cambridge, MA: Perseus.

Herzog, C., Kramer, A.F., Wilson, R.S., & Lindenberger, U. (2008). Enrichment effects on adult development. *Psychological Science in the Public Interest, 9,* 1-65.

Hillier, S.M., & Barrow, G.M. (2011). *Aging, the individual, and society* (9th ed.). Belmont, CA: Wadsworth Cengage Learning.

Hooyman, N.R., & Kiyak, H.A. (2011). *Social gerontology: A multidisciplinary perspective* (9th ed.). Boston, MA: Allyn & Bacon/Pearson Education.

Jeste, D., et al. (2010). Neurocognitive disorders: A proposal from the DSM-5 Neurocognitive Disorders Work Group (draft 1/7/10). Washington, DC: American Psychiatric Association. Retrieved from http://www.DSM5.org

Kennedy, G.J. (2010, November 8). Proposed revisions of dementia diagnostic criteria for DSM-5. *Psychiatric Weekly,* 5(27). Retrieved from http://www.psychweekly.com

Kitwood, T. (1993). Towards a theory of dementia care: The interpersonal process. *Ageing & Society, 13,* 51-67.

Lindenberger, U., & von Oertzen, T. (2006). Variability in cognitive aging: From taxonomy to theory. In E. Bialystok & F.I.M. Craik (Eds.). *Lifespan cognition: Mechanisms of change* (Ch. 21). New York, NY: Oxford University Press.

Lockenhoff, C.E., & Carstensen, L.L. (2004). Socioemotional selectivity theory, aging, and health: The increasingly delicate balance between regulating emotions and making tough choices. *Journal of Personality, 72*(6), 1395-1424. doi: 10.1111/j.1467-6494.2004.00301.x

Miller, N.B., Smerglia, V. L., & Bouchet, N. (Winter, 2004). Women's adjustment to widowhood: Does social support matter? *Journal of Women and Aging, 16*(3/4), 149-167.

Roediger, III, H.L., & Karpicke, J.D. (2006). The power of testing memory: Basic research and implications for educational practice. *Perspectives on Psychological Science, 1*(3), 181-210. doi: 10.1111/j.1745-6916.2006.00012x

Rusted, J., Ratner, H., & Sheppard, L. (1995). When all else fails, we can still make tea: A longitudinal look at activities of daily living in an Alzheimer patient. In R. Campbell & M. Conway (Eds.), *Broken memories.* Oxford, UK: Blackwell.

Rusted, J., & Sheppard, L. (2002). Action-based memory in Alzheimer's disease: A longitudinal look at tea making. *Neurocase, 8,* 111-126.

Schaie, K.W. (2005). What can we learn from longitudinal studies of adult intellectual development? *Research in Human Development, 2*(3), 133-158.

Seifert, L.S. (1999). Charades as cognitive aids for individuals with probable Alzheimer's disease. *Clinical Gerontologist, 20,* 3-14.

Seifert, L.S. (2007). *Chasing dragonflies: Life and care in aging.* Cuyahoga Falls, OH: Clove Press LTD.

Seifert, L.S. (2009). *Roses grow in a butterfly garden: Stories and cognitive activities for elders life and how they work.* Cuyahoga Falls, Ohio: Clove Press LTD.

Seifert, L.S., & Baker, M.K. (1998). Procedural skills and art production among individuals with Alzheimer's-type dementia. *Clinical Gerontologist, 20,* 3-14.

Seifert, L.S., & Baker, M.K. (2003). Art and Alzheimer-type dementia: A longitudinal study. *Clinical Gerontologist, 26*(1/2), 3-15.

Seifert, L.S., & Baker, M.K. (2009). A report about current research: Maintenance of cognitive skills in persons with Alzheimer-type dementia. In L.S. Seifert, *Roses grow in a butterfly garden* (Ch. 6). Cuyahoga Falls, OH: Clove Press LTD.

Seifert, L.S., & Jones, A. (2011). Reviving slideshows: Technology and cognitive enrichment in dementia care. *Activities Directors' Quarterly, 11*(4).

Simard, J. (2007). *The end-of-life Namaste care program for people with dementia.* Baltimore, MD: Health Professions Press.

Smerglia, V.L. (2000). Caregiving. In P. Roberts, (Ed.), *Aging.* Pasadena, CA: Salem Press.

Smerglia, V.L., & Deimling, G.T. (1997). Care-related decision making satisfaction and caregiver well-being in families caring for older members. *The Gerontologist, 37*(5), 658-665.

Smerglia, V.L., Deimling, G.T., & Schaefer, M. (2001). The impact of race on decision-making satisfaction and caregiver depression: A path analytic model. *Journal of Mental Health and Aging, 7*(3), 301-316.

Smerglia, V., Miller, N. B., Sotnak, D. L., & Geiss, C. A. (2007). Social support and adjustment to caring for elder family members: A multi-study analysis. *Journal of Aging and Mental Health (International), 11*(2), 205-217.

Tun, P.A. (1998). Fast noisy speech: Age differences in processing rapid speech with background noise. *Psychology & Aging, 13,* 424-434.

Verhaeghen, P. (2003). Aging and vocabulary scores: A meta-analysis. *Psychology & Aging, 18,* 332-339.

Vygotsky, L.S. (1926/1997). *Educational psychology.* Delray Beach, FL: St. Lucie Press.

General Footnotes

Chapter 1

1. A "mixed group" includes two or more levels of functioning among its participants. For example, an activity session with normal functioning elders and some with Alzheimer-type dementia would be "mixed."

Chapter 2
None

Chapter 3

1. Lauren has seen numerous versions of this saying but was unable to discover to whom the original idea is attributed. For Lauren, who has a lovely sister, the saying seems to make sense!

Index of Terms

Activities,
    applications and examples, Chapters 1, 2, 3
    Five Big Hints activity, Chapter 1
    for elders with dementia, See discussion in Chapter 1,
        with examples in Chapters 2, 3
    for elders without cognitive impairment, Chapter 2
    for groups, Chapters 2, 3
    person-centered (individual), Chapter 1
    short stories and discussion, Chapters 2, 3
Alzheimer's disease (AD), Chapter 1

Caregiver/Caregiving, Chapter 1

"Domains of Contact", see "Ways of Making Contact" in Chapter 1

Interventions (in eldercare),
    cognitive, Chapter 1
    general; See "Activities" above
    hierarchy of, Appendix
    memory & cognitive tasks, Chapter 1
    storytelling, Chapters 1, 2, 3
    storytelling techniques, Chapters 1, 2, 3

Longitudinal research,
    cognitive maintenance, Chapter 1

Memory,
    information & tasks for aging memory are abundant in this book, Chapters 1, 2, 3

"Neurocognitive Impairment"
    defined and compared to "dementia", Chapter 1

PADding,
    "practicing against decline" from dementia, Chapter 1
Person-centered care,
    Kitwood, Chapter 1

Principles in memory activities,
    the Six-Week Rule, Chapter 1

Sensory systems,
    and aging, Chapter 1
Short stories,
    for individuals and groups, Chapters 2, 3
    with "Talking Points", Chapters 2, 3
Subject-performed tasks, Chapter 1